DISNEP
ARTEMIS FOWL

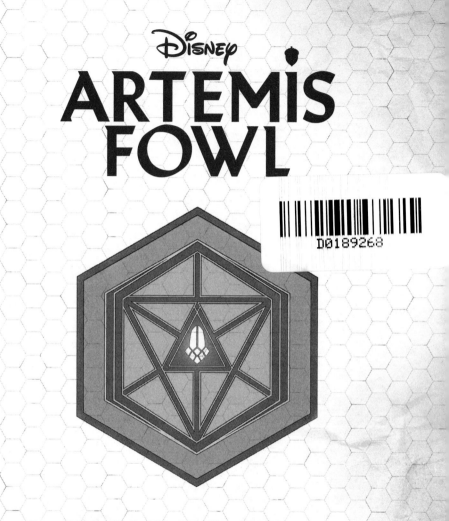

D0189268

HOW TO BE A
L.E.P.RECON

DISNEP
ARTEMIS
FOWL

HOW TO BE A
L.E.P.RECON

YOUR GUIDE TO THE GEAR, GADGETS, AND GOINGS-ON
OF THE WORLD'S MOST ELITE FAIRY FORCE

WRITTEN BY MATTHEW K. MANNING
ILLUSTRATED BY ANDRÉ PELAES
AND CARLOS TRON

BASED ON THE NOVELS
BY EOIN COLFER

DISNEP PRESS

LOS ANGELES · NEW YORK

Copyright © 2019 Disney Enterprises, Inc.
All rights reserved. Published by Disney Press, an imprint of Disney Book Group. No part of this book may be reproduced or transmitted in any form or by any means, electronic or mechanical, including photocopying, recording, or by any information storage and retrieval system, without written permission from the publisher. For information address Disney Press, 1200 Grand Central Avenue, Glendale, California 91201.

Printed in the United States of America
First Paperback Edition, June 2019

1 3 5 7 9 10 8 6 4 2

FAC-026988-19130

Library of Congress Control Number: 2019935580

ISBN 978-1-368-04126-3

Designed by Gegham Vardanyan

For more Disney Press fun,
visit www.disneybooks.com

CONTENTS

Introduction 6

Chapter One: **THE UNDERGROUND** 14

Chapter Two: **CITIZENS OF THE UNDERGROUND** 37

Chapter Three: **CAUTIONARY TALE #1** 76

Chapter Four: **DEPARTMENTS OF THE L.E.P.** 92

Chapter Five: **STAFF OF THE L.E.P.** 103

Chapter Six: **CAUTIONARY TALE #2** 136

Chapter Seven: **STAYING IN SHAPE** 145

Chapter Eight: **L.E.P. TRANSPORT** 152

Chapter Nine: **L.E.P. GEAR AND GADGETS** 172

Chapter Ten: **CAUTIONARY TALE #3** 199

Chapter Eleven: **SURFACE LOCATIONS OF NOTE** 208

Chapter Twelve: **MUD PEOPLE TO AVOID AT ALL COSTS!** . . . 222

Conclusion 232

Addendum: Gnommish-to-English Translation Key . . 236

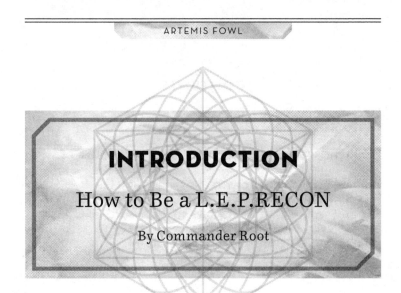

INTRODUCTION
How to Be a L.E.P.RECON

By Commander Root

As acting commander of the Lower Elements Police Reconnaissance (or L.E.P.recon), I have become aware that many of the members of my force aren't as well versed in police procedure as they should be.

This has been a banner year for foul-ups, and yes, I use that term with every bit of the pun intended. The most egregious of these foul-ups? A human made contact with the fairy folk against our will. He read our book. He fooled us. This Artemis Fowl, as he's called, is a Mud Person know-it-all, and I, for one, would be happier if he knew-it-much-less. He showed us our weaknesses.

For that reason, and because there have been so many intradepartmental arguments and general mistakes both on the streets and above them, I've decided to write this manual.

Trust me, I'm no happier about it than you are.

Right off the bat, I want to stress that this manual is in no way a replacement for *The Booke of the People*. As you should be aware, that particular tome sets in place every rule and regulation that must be followed by *every* fairy, day in and day out, with no exceptions.

Commander Root,

Per your request, I've compiled my thoughts on this first draft of How to Be a L.E.P.recon. I have to admit, however, you've kind of put me in an awkward position. I'm worried that if I offer an honest critique, I might offend you. Now that I'm finally a captain, I'm in no hurry to be demoted.

But I've given it my best shot. Just remember: you asked for this!

Here goes nothing. . . .

—Captain Holly Short

On the day of their birth, no matter their station or fairy association, a newborn fairy is given a copy of this text. It details our laws, our history, and our magic. It is the most important tome in all of the fairy world. It is sacred. It is law. And among the many jobs of an L.E.P. officer is upholding the laws put forth in that most sacred tome.

Don't you think this introduction could be . . . what's the word I'm looking for . . . I don't know, friendlier?

Just a thought.

Please don't fire me.

—HS

This book, on the other hand, is meant to serve as a starting point for your career here at the L.E.P. And yes, that means this book is going to deliver a hearty second serving of guidelines. Complainers can expect to be reassigned to a position at the North Pole. And if you think I'm a tough boss, wait until you meet the guy in charge up there.

L.E.P. officers must hold themselves to a higher standard than your average fairy on the street. The Lower Elements Police must put courtesy before all else when dealing with civilians. And remember: fairies do

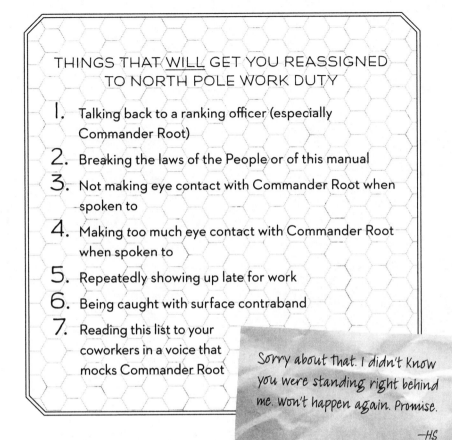

THINGS THAT WILL GET YOU REASSIGNED TO NORTH POLE WORK DUTY

1. Talking back to a ranking officer (especially Commander Root)
2. Breaking the laws of the People or of this manual
3. Not making eye contact with Commander Root when spoken to
4. Making too much eye contact with Commander Root when spoken to
5. Repeatedly showing up late for work
6. Being caught with surface contraband
7. Reading this list to your coworkers in a voice that mocks Commander Root

Sorry about that. I didn't know you were standing right behind me. Won't happen again. Promise.

—HS

not consort with human beings from the surface. Those Mud People are to be avoided at all times.

You'd think I wouldn't have to remind you of this sort of thing, but here we are.

Inside this manual you'll find not just a set of rules

THE BOOKE OF THE PEOPLE

that *must* be followed to the letter, but also a refresher on fairy history, variety, locations, and technology. You'll meet some of our staff, hear harrowing stories from the field, and learn more about the inner workings of the L.E.P. than you ever wanted to know. (Tough

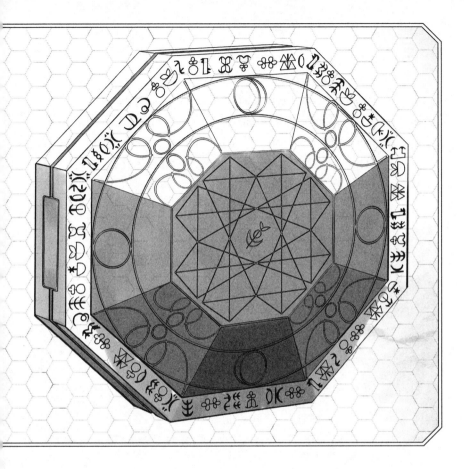

luck, Officer. Put on your big-fairy pants.) It's my hope that this manual will help our fine organization become more of a well-oiled machine and less of a complete and total embarrassment when I have to present my monthly report to the Fairy Council.

I'll conclude with a passage from *The Booke of the People*. It's one you should all know by heart, but I can't be too sure of anything these days, apparently. Let's just put it this way: if you don't know these words by now, you'd better have them memorized by the next time we see each other. You will be tested.

***

Carry me always, carry me well.
I am thy teacher of herb and spell.
I am thy link to power arcane.
Forget me and thy magick shall wane.

Ten times ten commandments there be.
They will answer every mystery.
Cures, curses, alchemy,
These secrets shall be thine, through me.

But, Fairy, remember this above all:
I am not for those in mud that crawl.
And forever doomed shall be the one
Who betrays my secrets one by one.

And that goes double for the L.E.P., recruits!

Commander Root

L.E.P. HEADQUARTERS, HAVEN CITY

CHAPTER ONE

The Underground

A QUICK HISTORY LESSON

In ancient times, fairies were for the most part surface dwellers. We could fly through the relatively fresh air, feel the moon's glow on our skin, and live joyfully in forests, with few, if any, natural predators. Then came the Mud People.

In short order, they stank up the air, dirtied the ground, and polluted our streams. Their industry mowed down our forests with little to no thought of the conservation of the planet's natural resources. Simply put, Mud People found no reason to replace what they

PROS AND CONS OF LIFE IN THE UNDERGROUND

PROS

◉ Privacy from Mud People

◉ Water is always warm due to position near the Earth's core.

◉ You can relax your troubles away in any number of exclusive springs—our very own natural spas!

◉ Man-made pollutants are filtered out.

◉ No rain or snow to make you tardy for work at the L.E.P.

◉ Privacy from Mud People (It warrants repeating!)

CONS

◉ Manufactured air just can't compare to the air up there.

◉ Plenty of unintentional rhyming

◉ Small living quarters (Most residents live in homes roughly the size of a human phone booth.)

◉ None of those little chocolate eggs with the toys inside (Why don't we have those, anyway?)

You know, if our ever-so-generous commander felt like giving her officers a raise, we might be able to afford a place bigger than a closet....

—Captain Holly Short

stole. It became a world of man, and fairies were forced to retreat inside the very Earth to survive.

It was about ten thousand years ago when magic fled the surface. The Underground is now the last human-free zone we know of. Here we can filter out the pollutants of the Mud People and travel about freely without having to worry about shielding ourselves from the vision of those who would seek to do us harm. We have built tremendous eco-friendly industries operating out of our great cities. And there's no city in the Underground quite like Haven City, the one I call home.

PLACES TO BE:
WHAT IS WHERE IN HAVEN CITY

HAVEN CITY

A natural hub, with chutes leading to some of the most exotic and popular destinations on the surface, Haven City is the largest city in the Underground. The population here is as diverse as anywhere in, or on, the planet. Elves, goblins, dwarfs. You name it, we've got way too many of them. As an officer, you will quickly learn that overcrowding is one of the main causes of strife in our communities.

Not only is the city populated with fairies who live and work here, it's also crammed with tourists. From garden-variety gnomes to sprites taking in the sights, the city is full of not just pedestrians but flying transport vehicles as well. I'm not sure why visitors feel the need to bring their own cumbersome modes of transportation, but it is rather irksome. Parking violation tickets and speeding tickets are encouraged.

THE THOROUGHFARE

Getting into, out of, and through Haven City can be a challenge due to the aforementioned population problem. The Thoroughfare is the main route of travel in the city, but it has more congestion than a dwarf on a limestone-only diet. We're talking over four lanes of traffic going each direction. (And one of those directions is straight up.)

Word of advice: give yourself extra time if you plan on taking the Thoroughfare to work, even if you're

HAVEN CITY

just winging it. The city center is always especially crowded, so plan your schedule accordingly. Officers wear moonometers for a reason. You should always be aware of what time it is, as the L.E.P. needs to run as efficiently as possible. Tardiness is not something we look kindly on.

Isn't that right, Captain Short?

OKay. Hold it.

Isn't this supposed to be an "official" document? I don't think that last bit was necessary. How about next time you send me an email rather than air your grievances to the entire police department? Just a thought. And seriously, just a thought. If you want to make this have a more personal touch, I get it. Please, just really don't fire me.

—Captain Holly Short

THE FOUNTAIN OF YOUTH

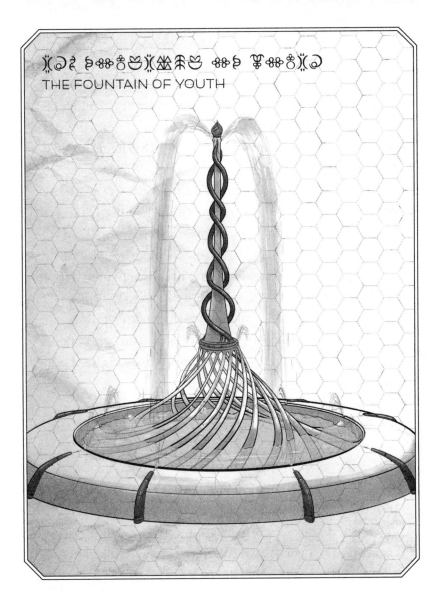

THE FOUNTAIN OF YOUTH

As you can imagine, the Fountain is our biggest tourist attraction. It brings in all types of fairies from all types of places, and wait times can be long. This leads not just to traffic issues, but to general unrest. While waiting to get a glimpse of the famous water and the many, many coins that litter the bottom of this little pool, fairies have been known to become rather impatient. Talking leads to yelling; yelling leads to pushing; pushing leads to shoving. Pretty soon you have whole families of gnomes poking each other with their sharp little hats. If you've ever worked Fountain detail, you know it's never pretty. So when the time comes to do a stint there, don't look at it as an easy day. You will need to be vigilant and hyperaware.

And don't get me started on the prices they charge for the photo ops! That, if you ask me, is the real crime.

SPUD'S SPUD EMPORIUM

If you have a taste for fast food—and most everybody does—then there's nothing like a greasy bag of fries from Spud's. Sure, it's another crowded tourist spot, but a fairy can't live on salads alone.

TOP FIVE ITEMS
AT SPUD'S SPUD EMPORIUM

1. **GOBLIN BURGER WITH EXTRA GREASE**—a sloppy flame-broiled mess

2. **DIRT DEVIL DOG**—recommended for dwarfs (or those other rare few who enjoy a heaping helping of mud on their hot dog)

3. **COVERED AND SMOTHERED SPUDS**—best not to ask what the fries are covered and smothered with

4. **SPRITE SHAKE**—warning: contains glitter. Drink at your own risk!

5. **THE ROOT CANAL**—the sweetest soda in the Underground, named after L.E.P.'s own Commander Root

Yum. Now I'm hungry. If you're making a food run, I'll take a double order of spuds and a small Root Canal. Okay, make it an extra large. (It's my cheat day.)

—HS

HOWLER'S PEAK

Not all the sights in Haven City are picturesque. Some
are terrifying prisons meant for the worst ilk of fairy
that society has to offer. Case in point? Howler's Peak.

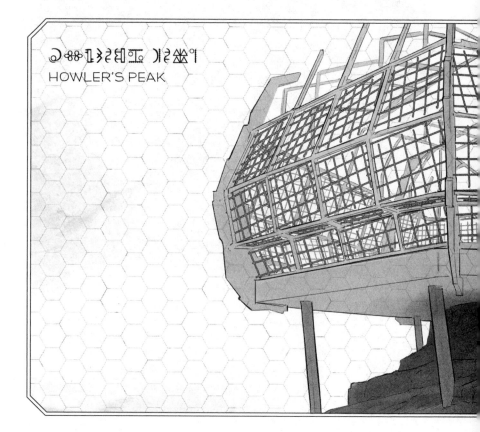

HOWLER'S PEAK

This prison holds the worst of the worst. There is no room for softness at Howler's. Once you pass through the gates, you very rarely get to go back out them.

If you're on prison detail, it can be an easy gig,

WANTED

ARMED AND VERY DANGEROUS

REWARD 10,000

helping transport shackled fairies from point A to point B. A boring gig, sure, but an easy one. But be careful. Howler's has an effect on fairies. More than one officer has fallen victim to the doom and gloom of the prison. Don't linger. Just remember: the prison serves as a warning of what happens if you break the laws of the People. Try not to dwell on what goes on inside.

FAIRY COUNCIL HEADQUARTERS

You can't have a council without giving its members a place to hold it. The Fairy Council Headquarters is quite an impressive building. Our tax dollars at work, I guess. Why spend any money paving over those potholes on the Thoroughfare when you can give our elected officials nicer amenities in the council bathrooms? Not that any-one is asking me, and I order you to keep these musings to yourself.

A dozen of the most elite fairies make up our lovely council, whether I want them to or not. The group meets in their star-shaped chambers, their every decision and budgetary meeting recorded for posterity and played back ad nauseam, thanks to monitors larger than the council's own ego spaced around all of Haven City.

You may be getting the impression that the Fairy Council HQ is not my favorite spot in the city to visit. But I don't know what would give you that idea.

POLICE HEADQUARTERS

Police Headquarters. Located within Police Plaza in Haven City, it is truly the most important building in all the Underground. Without it, our world would have descended into chaos long ago. While nothing special to look at (that would be the Fairy Council stealing the thunder—again), our headquarters house the best, the brightest, the

COMMANDER ROOT'S OFFICE

strongest, and the bravest. Each room within headquarters serves a unique purpose. Decades upon decades of those whose job is to uphold the law and provide safety to the Underground have shaped this place. True, the past few years have put some strain on headquarters. But I have faith that the building, and the symbol of hope it provides, will be standing long after I am gone.

POLICE PLAZA

Good way to drum up some pride in the workplace! Doesn't matter how many times I walk up to that door— still get chills.

—Captain Holly Short

Note: I encourage new officers to explore headquarters. But do not—I repeat: do not—think my office should also be part of that tour. While I think of it as the heart of Central Command, my office is a place you'd better hope to visit as little as possible. It should be noted that they have virtually soundproofed the walls to allow me to express my . . . displeasure . . . from time to time with my staff.

In addition to the myriad types of high-tech equipment at our disposal, I've asked Foaly to set up view screens to give me eyes everywhere I need them, and the multiple phone lines to different departments allow me to touch base with even the most remote L.E.P. locations. I like to keep my finger on the pulse of Haven City, and my office allows me to do just that.

CENTRAL COMMAND AND FOALY'S OFFICE

Central Command is made up of a variety of offices and workstations. As the name implies, Central Command is where all commands come from. While my office is the most important, the other offices are vital to the day-to-day running of HQ. Chief among those is Foaly's office. It is here that Foaly uses his satellites to piggyback relays

FOALY'S OFFICE

from all over the surface and project them onto his giant plasma screens. I'd say this is where the magic happens when it comes to his many technological advancement

CENTRAL COMMAND

ideas, but Foaly is anything but magic. It's more appropriate to say that this is where the science happens.

Science, and way too many backhanded comments.

RULES FOR VISITING FOALY'S OFFICE UNINVITED

RULE #1: DON'T VISIT FOALY'S OFFICE UNINVITED.
RULE #2: MISS RULE #1, DID YA?

HOLDING CELLS

No police headquarters would be complete without a decent-sized holding cell. This is where we keep our perps and suspected perps until they're ready for release or transfer to Howler's Peak. If you ever find yourself working the cells, make sure you follow one general rule: do not mix certain fairy types! Having goblins and dwarfs share a cell is just asking for trouble.

While there are many metropolises sprinkled throughout the Underground, Haven City remains a shining star. Like any city, it has its pluses and minuses, but when you get right down to the nitty-gritty, it is the booming—and safe—metropolis it is thanks to the dedicated officers of the L.E.P.

CHAPTER TWO

Citizens of the Underground

THE BROAD WORLD OF FAIRIES

Unless you've been living under a rock your whole life—and yes, I'm aware some fairies actually enjoy living under rocks—you've realized that there are quite a few different kinds of fairy folk. A common misconception among Mud People is that fairies are a different breed of creature than, say, centaurs. But we in the Underground understand that the word "fairy" is a general term. We're all fairies in one way or another.

However, under the large umbrella of the term "fairy" is a multitude of subspecies. It is these subspecies that differentiate fairy folk. These categories group us based on our physical attributes, abilities, and the like. Now I know there are many different combinations out there—like those who are half elf, half gnome, for example. But to form an understanding of the People as a whole, it's important to examine some of the traits unique to each species. This knowledge will help you in the field as well. As they say, the best way to defeat your enemy is to know your enemy. And sometimes, unfortunately, our enemies are ourselves.

But getting back to fairies in general . . .

While some species are exempt from this rule, fairies are on average three feet, one centimeter in height. That's the average, mind you, and it doesn't account for the phenomenal growth of some more radical Underground dwellers.

Fairies in general are not fans of natural light. We haven't operated in the sun for centuries, in fact. The eternal twilight of the Underground is what most are used to, as even fairies on vacation visit the surface mainly at night.

This aversion to natural light is partly because some fairy folk burn rather easily in the sun's rays. But more important, *all* of us find it hard to operate at full magic when caught in the bright light of day. Simply put, the sun dilutes magic. As an L.E.P. officer, you have a duty to avoid excess sunlight whenever possible. So no beach days.

Also, fairies in general can have a child only about once every twenty years. Here at the L.E.P., officers who are also parents aren't frowned upon. We welcome the chance to pass on L.E.P. principles and morals to the next generation. But keep in mind police work is often dangerous work. Even if you have a child once every two decades, that's a lot of little ones who would miss you if things got too rough in the line of duty.

> Great. Now what am I supposed to do with this new swimsuit? Just Kidding! I Know the rules. I would never do something like impulsively buy a swimsuit on sale for no reason other than I liked the pattern. Never.
>
> —Captain Holly Short

THE FAIRY SUBSPECIES

As I mentioned before, fairy-kind is divided into many subspecies. While it's always a mistake to stereotype, each fairy group has certain traits and abilities. To become an L.E.P. officer functioning at the top of your game, you need to understand the powers and natural tendencies that each magical creature possesses. As I mentioned, it will help you know what to expect when backed into a corner by an angry goblin or when pursing a dwarf through a bedrock tunnel.

There are sure to be those members of a species who break the mold, but more often than not, you can use your knowledge about fairy folk to help turn the tables on your opponents, understand their motives, or predict their next moves.

ELVES

While not the largest or strongest of the subspecies, elves are the most populous of the fairies. They are what most Mud People picture when they think of the fairy world, and have been represented—correctly *and* incorrectly—in the Mud People's entertainment culture.

Small and able to be picked out of a lineup by their pointy ears, if nothing else, elves have a variety of jobs in Underground society. Their personalities range from

chipper to grumpy, and their little fingers are perfect for everything from deftly handling L.E.P.-issue technology to assembling toys in colder climates.

Elves typically have brown or tan skin and red hair. But over the ages, this has become less consistent due to more elf-gnome families sprinkling the Underground.

Elves are a proud and loyal bunch known for their intelligence, strong moral code, and sarcastic—yet deeply witty—sense of humor. Gifted with several types of magic—such as the power to heal themselves and others and the ability to make themselves invisible and use Mesmer—they also have the gift of tongues. This allows them to speak any language and makes them particularly useful in trade negotiations.

Fond of flying, they are perhaps the best natural aviators in the world, despite what the sprites would have you believe.

I second that!

—HS

CENTAURS

There's an old saying that it's easy to tell when a centaur is in the room—he'll tell you. Accurate ancient clichés aside, centaurs are indeed rather easy to identify. Their top half is that of a man or woman, the bottom half that of a pony. They've got four hooves that are prone to bouts of uncomfortable dryness, and they have much more hair than a typical fairy.

CENTAUR

Lucky for the rest of us, there are very few of them left in existence. Trust me, the over-the-top personality of the ones who do remain more than makes up for the loss of the rest of their species. Centaurs have incredibly inflated egos. They believe they are the smartest fairies in the room, no matter what the room, and they will tell you so right away. In addition, they adore a good intellectual debate if it means they can follow it up with a lively round of boasting. Nevertheless, most actually are quite adept with technology and inventive, like our very own Officer Foaly.

Centaurs can also be a bit paranoid. That could be because they possess absolutely no magic whatsoever. I guess it's natural to always be looking over your shoulder if you have no way to heal it offhand. Honestly, I'm surprised Foaly doesn't wear a tinfoil hat.

Don't give him any ideas!

—HS

PIXIES

It can be difficult to tell a pixie from an elf at first glance. Both are about three feet tall, and both have pointy ears. Pixies, however, have a more human appearance, especially when they style their hair over their ears to mask those pesky aforementioned points.

PIXIE

Like elves, pixies possess some magic. They, too, can speak any language and have the gift of Mesmer. However, their tendency to use magic for silly tricks can make other fairies look down on their abilities.

One thing is consistent among all pixies: they love

power, money, and chocolate. They are extremely cunning and ambitious, and some say they lack most morals, if not all of them. I'm not sure I agree with that harsh assessment, but I don't let my guard down around any pixies in my general vicinity; that's for sure.

Who are you trying to fool? You don't let your guard down around anyone!

—Captain Holly Short

SPRITES

There are those who say that fairies evolved from flying dinosaurs or birds. I believe sprites are what fuel that school of thinking. While they're often much too busy bragging about their still-attached natural wings, sprites love to say that they climbed a different evolutionary ladder from the rest of us whenever they can insert that information into the conversation.

Around a yard tall with pointy ears, like their pixie and elf cousins, sprites usually have green skin. So if

SPRITE

the wings didn't give them away, the skin should. They possess average intelligence and above-average ego. They think of themselves as beautiful and do not seem bothered by their very limited magical abilities (they can heal minor wounds, but not major ones), making up for it with abundant pride in their exceptionally speedy reflexes.

The most notable thing about sprites is that they adore flying perhaps more than any other fairy. I don't know how many sprites I've personally brought into Police Headquarters for reckless flying through Haven City.

GNOMES

There's a tendency in Haven City to think that all gnomes are tourists. Residents think that these usually short and rather dull creatures come from remote parts of the Underground to gawk at our various tall buildings and popular landmarks. There's also a general school of thought that says that all gnomes are country bumpkins who are better off in a flyover part of the world than in the way of busy fairies who just want to get to work on time. Some say that they can't wait around while gnomes dig through their oversized trousers for a coin for the city transport. Yes, there are those who think these negative things about gnomes every single day of the year.

GNOME

And that's all I'm going to say on the subject of gnomes. Oh, and I recommend avoiding them. In general. Because they will just get in your way. They are too slow to be a danger of any kind and their magic is barely existent. Really, that's all I'm going to say. . . .

Moving on . . .

—HS

TROLLS

These nonmagical behemoths are not your average fairy folk. Usually as big as a baby elephant (some can grow up to 397 pounds!) and not nearly as smart, trolls are the meanest of the deep-tunnel creatures. The list of things they like is dwarfed by the list of things they hate. Their eyes and ears are quite sensitive, but their retractable claws and rows upon rows of teeth certainly make up for any perceived weaknesses.

Trolls are hairy, and most have bulky green tongues. Some trolls even have tusks like a wild boar's. If you find yourself on the sharp end of those tusks, your body won't experience pain from impalement, but euphoria. The tusks release a sort of numbing agent

TROLL

that keeps the troll's victim happy and docile. It makes finishing the job that much easier for these always-hungry monsters.

Trolls are exceptionally strong but do have the tiniest of weak spots located at the base of their skulls. This

THINGS TROLLS HATE

⬡ Bright light

⬡ Loud noise

⬡ Other fairies getting in their way

⬡ Pain of any kind

⬡ You, probably

can be used to your advantage . . . if you dare get that close to a troll—which I try to avoid if at all possible.

Any amount of discomfort or pain can cause a troll to go from a destructive beast on a walk to a destructive beast on a rampage. This is why we in the L.E.P. do our best to keep trolls happy, even those in police custody.

L.E.P. Recon and Retrieval teams are often called into action when a troll escapes the Underground by accidentally riding up a pressure elevator or dormant volcano. They're tough enough that they can survive such trips. But they never arrive on the surface without experiencing enough pain to make them way too hot to handle for a single L.E.P. officer. Oftentimes even a dozen L.E.P.

officers are not able to handle them. I cannot stress it enough: trolls should be treated with the utmost caution.

Trolls may be nonmagical, but that doesn't stop them from being extremely deadly. Last quarter alone, the L.E.P. lost six officers to troll attacks. And that wasn't even a busy quarter!

TOOLS TO TAKE DOWN TROLLS

Trolls are allergic to wasp juice and nettles, but a concoction of the stuff won't incapacitate them. On the contrary: the concoction does just the opposite. The juice makes them twice as mad and twice as strong. (Don't ask me how I know this. You don't want the answer.) So do not attempt to use it.

Coordinated attacks are best when dealing with a rogue troll. When that doesn't work, there's always the time-honored tradition of crawling under a table and hiding. I'm not suggesting L.E.P. officers actually hide from trouble. But I figure you should at least know all your options.

After my recent experiences, the less I think about trolls, the better.

—HS

GOBLINS AND DWARFS

Anyone who has spent time in the L.E.P. should be well versed in these two particular subspecies. The goblin–dwarf turf war isn't just something that grabs headlines in the *Underground Gazette*. Curbing these fights is one of our most dangerous—and time-consuming—assignments.

Over the years, Haven City has seen more than its fair share of goblin-on-dwarf violence and vice versa. And the interactions are on the rise. As commander, I've seen more than most. There have been goblins who have worked alone, trying to infiltrate a particular dwarf's home and wreak havoc on his life. And there have been instances in which thousands of goblins have taken to the street, looking for any sign of a dwarf or a dwarf sympathizer with the sheer goal of doing as much damage to as many of them as they can. Either way, it isn't pretty. Or safe.

GOBLINS

So let's talk about goblins first. These guys are scaly; that's something you notice right off the bat. But it's their scaly, slimy skin that allows them to be fireproof—on the outside, at least. The inside is a different story.

GOBLIN

Goblins need to be fireproof because they have the magical ability to create and hurl fireballs. When it comes to crime and gang-related incidents, this certainly ups the number of arson cases in the L.E.P. files. It gives goblins an instant leg up, and they should always be considered armed and dangerous.

Goblins have lidless eyes and a forked tongue. But the scales are probably enough for you to be able to identify one. Goblins also can cover ground fairly quickly because of their ability to run on all fours as naturally as a centaur, making them especially hard to catch if they get the chance to slip away.

The good thing is goblins aren't too clever. You'll never find one behind a string of heists, for instance.

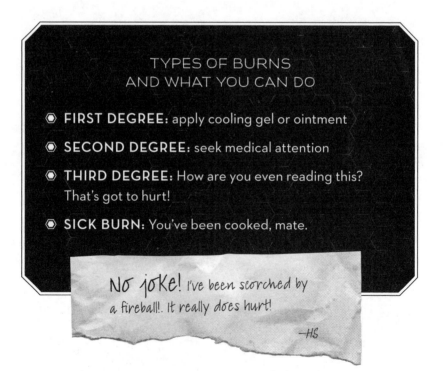

TYPES OF BURNS
AND WHAT YOU CAN DO

⬡ **FIRST DEGREE:** apply cooling gel or ointment

⬡ **SECOND DEGREE:** seek medical attention

⬡ **THIRD DEGREE:** How are you even reading this? That's got to hurt!

⬡ **SICK BURN:** You've been cooked, mate.

No joke! I've been scorched by a fireball!. It really does hurt!

—HS

They're prone to following leaders if those leaders can get them what they want—and what they want is usually a dwarf. Or revenge on a dwarf. They'll also turn on each other without a moment's notice, so it's important to keep a sharp eye on any lawbreaking members of their ilk.

Know this is probably not the kind of note you had in mind, but . . . have you tried that BBQ joint on Fifth Street? Say what you will about goblins, but they can certainly smoke a brisket! Those guys know their way around a fire.

—Captain Holly Short

DWARFS

On the other side of the goblin–dwarf rift are, as you might have guessed, dwarfs. Do not be mistaken: while dwarfs are often the victims in these battles, criminal dwarfs are just as much to blame as criminal goblins.

Dwarfs have a definite advantage in the world due to their ability to appear harmless at first sight. They're usually short, round, and a bit hairy. While their magical abilities are limited to the gift of tongues, when you take a peek inside their mouths, you can see how their natural talents are powerful enough.

DWARF

These guys are natural chompers. Sure, the dwarfs I know like to use their mouths to talk as much as dig, but their burrowing skills set them apart from the rest of fairy-kind. They are able to unhinge their jaws, allowing their big tombstone teeth to do their work, grinding away at anything from loose earth to solid rock.

Given these abilities, most law-abiding dwarfs are miners by trade. They can ingest several pounds of dirt per second, and they possess a super metabolism that allows them to quickly process the earth they take in. Yes, that means when tunneling, a dwarf must undo the bum flap on his or her pants, allowing the processed dirt and stone to . . . er . . . exit. This can be a repulsive thing to witness. A word of warning: don't stand too close to a dwarf's behind.

Not only are dwarfs' tunnels self-sealing because of this ability to process dirt, but dwarfs are also prone to violent downward-shooting gas that could knock an elephant across a courtyard. Those inclined toward a life of crime often use this ability as a weapon, keeping a bit of reserve air in the tank, if you catch my drift.

But seriously, don't catch their drift!.

—HS

When underground, dwarfs steer themselves by using a type of sonar.

Many prefer to eat their way through dirt they've already eaten and digested, as it tends to be looser and allows them to travel quickly. However, this is a point of contention among dwarf-kind, as others view this practice of re-eating dirt pretty . . . well, gross.

Fortunately, for a species so easily able to tunnel to the surface, dwarfs have absolutely no interest in living aboveground among the Mud People, because of their heightened sensitivity to light and their complete and utter hatred of fire. Of course, it's that fear of fire that gives any goblin worth his salt an extreme advantage in a conflict with a dwarf.

To a dwarf, the sun is a giant ball of flame that is much too close for comfort. They have a burn time of less than three minutes if they're exposed to sunlight, so they're often forced to wear skintight blackout suits to compensate for their bodies' sensitivity.

Another strange dwarf trait is that these guys can drink through their skin. Yes, if thirsty enough, they could put their arm in a tub of water and gulp the whole thing down through their pores. This allows dwarfs to draw moisture from the dirt while digging. But when parched, dwarfs can use these opening pores as miniature suction cups, allowing them to stick to flat

KNOW YOUR DWARF BEARD

While often adorable, dwarf beards are also functional. Case in point:

◉ Their beard hair is actually a matrix of antennae that aid in navigation.

◉ The hairs can move independently, like tendrils.

◉ When plucked, the individual hairs become rigid and can be used to pick locks.

surfaces. So with their very skin, dwarfs can suction to glass and scale a building if they're in the mood to do such a crazy thing.

Bottom line? All these attributes and abilities mean one thing: if a dwarf adopts a life of crime, it's really hard to stop him or her. Trust me. Talk about a true pain in the rear.

GREMLINS

You know, there's really not too much to say about gremlins. These guys aren't the friendliest sort and are, in fact, rather stuck up. They are known to make quite a stink when they're on vacation or at a restaurant. If the world isn't revolving around gremlin-kind, then they'll certainly let you know about it. But then again, that can be said about most of us in this day and age.

Oh, that's right. Your cousin married a gremlin. I was wondering why you're mostly keeping mum on the subject. Somebody is trying to avoid an awkward holiday dinner. . . .

Not that there is anything wrong with that.

Right, I'll stick to more on-topic notes.

Still not going to fire me, right?

—Captain Holly Short

Now you know the main differences among the various fairy folk who populate the Underground. Learn the traits described here and memorize the distinctions.

GREMLIN

But also be very aware of the fact that each and every fairy might just be able to defy your expectations. Nobody in real life exactly matches his or her description on paper.

One thing you'll learn about working in the L.E.P. is that there's *always* room for surprises.

MAGIC

In addition to the differences in the various species, it is important to look at powers possessed by some—but not all—of the fairy folk. They separate the fairies from the Mud People, help our society thrive, and keep us protected in an ever more dangerous world.

HEALING

Before I explain healing, I need to remind you of an important part of the healing process—and this is the big one: power reserves. The last thing any fairy wants is to be out in the field with a magic reader at 1 percent while facing a debilitating injury. Keep your power reserves high, officers, because the only effective L.E.P. is a healthy L.E.P. And without power, there is no healing.

Healing is a natural ability of some types of fairy, and it's perhaps the most important power to those who have it. With a few blue sparks of energy, even the most life-threatening of injuries can be reversed if we have enough power at our disposal. Mending broken bones or torn tissue means a second chance at taking down whatever broke those bones or tore that tissue in the first place.

I feel like these power reserve comments are personal digs at me. I get it, I get it! I'll keep my magic levels high from now on. Geez, give an elf a break.

—HS

It also means something close to immortality. Fairies as a rule might be fine-boned and appear to be weak. And we might be small in general. But it's our power to heal

HOW TO TELL IF YOU'RE IN NEED OF HEALING

◉ One part of you is broken and/or missing

◉ More than one part of you is broken and/or missing

◉ Nearly all of you is broken and/or missing

◉ You drank your milkshake too fast and now you have a headache our own wounds that puts us on a level playing field with some of the toughest combatants the world has to offer.

And do not forget about our ability to heal others. That in particular is a power to use sparingly and wisely. We can't go around healing every Mud Person with a common cold for risk of being discovered. But we can make a difference when need be. We can save a life.

REMEMBER:
HOLY WATER IS DEADLY TO FAIRIES!

IF YOU INGEST HOLY WATER,
JUST ... DARE!

Don't panic!

All right, panic a little.

Remember your antidote. (A bit of spring water from a spot like Tara should do the trick!)

Eat a full meal to fill your empty stomach. (You've been vomiting a lot—trust us on this one.)

And life is precious—even a Mud Person's life. That's an idea every L.E.P. officer would do well to remember.

MESMER

Most fairies would say that Mesmer is the lowest form of magic. And most fairies would be right. It takes the least energy to pull off, and even some humans seem to possess a hint of the gift. But nevertheless, having the ability to use Mesmer is one of a fairy's greatest tools. It's also one of the cornerstones of defensive Lower Elements Police work.

By looking your target square in the eyes and speaking in a magic-filled voice that only fairies can produce, you, too, can convince an unsuspecting Mud Person to do your bidding—to an extent. You can't use Mesmer to break the rules put forth in *The Booke of the People*. And you can't use Mesmer to undermine the laws of polite society or the words of this very manual. What you *can* do is use Mesmer to exit a situation in which you've been spotted by a Mud Person and need a quick getaway. You can use Mesmer to calm an irate opponent. And you can use Mesmer to convince a human being that they never saw you in the first place.

Unfortunately, low-tech magic has low-tech solutions. That means if a human happens to be wearing a pair of special sunglasses—particularly polarized UV reflective lenses—then you're up a chute without a pod, and your Mesmer won't be effective. But very few Mud People know this trick, and you should be avoiding those who do anyway.

SUNGLASSES

If only I had been given the choice to avoid Artemis Fowl. . . .

—Captain Holly Short

SHIELDING

Another tried-and-true weapon in a magical fairy's arsenal is the ability to shield. Officer Foaly will be the first to tell you that shielding is a bit of a misnomer. But that's only because Foaly loves to correct other fairies.

Fairy shielding is, in actuality, the process of vibrating at a superfast frequency. This means that we're never in one place long enough to be detected by the human eye. At best, a Mud Person can see a bit of a shimmer in the air where we were last standing or flying. Even stealth-sensitive radar can't truly detect more than a tiny distortion when a fairy is actively using shielding.

Like any form of magic, using one's shields does take a bit of magical energy to execute. But in the plus column, it can be switched on nearly instantly if you've kept your magic levels where they should be. Just recite a short incantation from *The Booke of the People*, and— *bam*—instant vanishing act.

WINGS

As you may be aware—and if you are not, I suggest another reading of the *Booke*—fairies used to have more

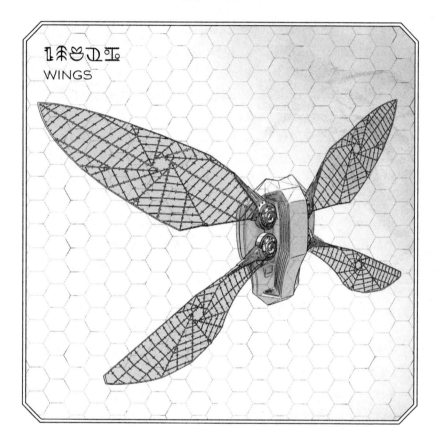

WINGS

abilities. Chief among those now absent powers was the ability to fly.

While our sprite brothers and sisters still retain their wings, all fairies used to have natural wings of their own. Whether they wasted away from evolution, disuse, or even some ancient curse remains open for debate. I am quite content with my police-issued artificial wings, but that's just me. I know many others, especially those of the younger generations, don't like being reliant on fake wings. Seems to me that fairies these days are always looking for something to complain about. I'm a proud believer in making the best of any given situation, even if that includes having to adapt to substandard wings due to budget cuts. But don't blame me. If you have a problem, take it up with the Fairy Council.

Somebody sure got defensive there at the end. Don't want to pony up for that wing upgrade I requested, huh? Remember, this should be a neutral manual. Keep it in check.

Ha-ha. Just kidding. Don't know why I said that. Seriously, please, please, please don't fire me.

—HS

TYPES OF CONTRABAND

1. Mud People **MUSIC**

2. Mud People **TELEVISION PROGRAMS AND MOVIES**

3. Mud People **TOYS AND GAMES**

4. Mud People **CLOTHING**

5. Mud People **TOOLS**

6. Mud People **BOOKS**

7. **MUD PEOPLE**

Is this another jab? Not sure why else you'd put it here. . . .

—HS

GOLD

The more you journey to the surface and observe Mud People, the more you'll realize that many of them are stuck on one particular concept when it comes to fairies: the idea of fairy gold. If we were to take the Mud Person's word for it, then every fairy would be lugging around a pot of gold, anxious to tuck it away under a

FAIRY GOLD

rainbow at any given opportunity. You and I know that's simply not true. The back pain alone would make it impractical. But try telling that to a Mud Person.

I wish you'd repeat that rule more often. I'm not sure I've heard it enough.

—HS

(That's just a figure of speech. Don't actually try telling that to a Mud Person. Remember: humans are strictly off-limits!)

Mud People are certain that every fairy is worth way more than his or her weight in gold. And here at the L.E.P., that's technically true. While we don't cart gold around with us, there *is* quite a large reserve in the council's special bank. Gold is measured in ingots, which is, in layman's terms, a gold acorn, and it is not used for daily transactions. The Fairy Council parts with its gold only in the rarest of circumstances.

Of course, in those circumstances, if a Mud Person actually gets away with tricking a fairy out of any amount of gold, the Mud Person gets to keep it free and clear. No strings attached. But don't take my word for it. Just read this passage from *The Booke of the People*:

ꝛꝶ Ꝟꝏꝶ ꝺꝸꝸꝸ ꝺꝥꝸꝸ ꝓꝸꝸꝸꝸ ꝓꝶꝸꝞꝏꝸꝷ
ꝛꝸ ꝓꝸꝛꝞꝶ ꝸꝸꝶ ꝺꝥꝓꝛꝓꝸꝷ ꝸꝸꝷ ꝸꝥꝥꝛꝷꝸ ꝓꝶꝥꝥꝺꝸꝸꝷꝷ
Ꝟꝏꝶꝸ ꝞꝏꝥꝞ ꝓꝸꝸꝸꝸ ꝛꝥ ꝏꝛꝥ Ꝟꝸꝸ ꝸꝶꝶꝞ
ꝺꝸꝞꝛꝷ ꝏꝶ ꝸꝛꝶꝥ ꝛꝸ ꝸꝞꝸꝷꝥꝥꝸꝷ ꝓꝸꝶꝶꝞ.

If the Mud Man gold can gather,
In spite of magick or fairy glamour,
Then that gold is his to keep
Until he lies in eternal sleep.

While none of this would be a big deal if humans weren't so obsessed with their outdated stories, gold has become a major factor in human–fairy relations. And for the record, yes, there should be no such thing as human–fairy relations in the first place!

CHAPTER THREE

Cautionary Tale #1

TALE #1 TAKEAWAY:
FAIRIES MUST
NEVER BE SEEN
BY MUD PEOPLE.

In my long history with the L.E.P., I've found that cadets learn more through actual police work than by reading and rereading manuals and workbooks. Since this is, in fact, a manual, I thought it best to include some examples from the field, of fairies breaking a few of the cardinal rules of *The Booke of the People* and the consequences that resulted from those errors in judgment. This way, you can learn from others' mistakes without making your own on the L.E.P.'s dime.

The first lesson comes to you from a gnome by the name of Jeffrey Wigglebottom. Go ahead, get the laughing out of the way now. I've been on the force for centuries, haven't laughed out loud for over two hundred years, and even I had to stifle a giggle the first time I heard his name spoken out loud.

Are you good now? Okay. Then let's continue.

On a scheduled, and fully sanctioned, vacation to the surface, Wigglebottom got himself into a spot of trouble and broke the first rule of fairy folk.

You can let him get to the bottom of it himself, no ifs, ands, or butts about it.

Get it? Wigglebottom? C'mon, I bet you laughed. Or at least smiled.

—HS

DEFENDANT STATEMENT
LOWER ELEMENTS POLICE

INITIAL REPORT: #256-759-007-21

STATEMENT BY: JEFFREY WIGGLEBOTTOM

LOCATION: HOWLER'S PEAK, HAVEN CITY

My name is Jeffrey Wigglebottom, and for the record, no, I've never understood why that's funny. I've been asked to write my best account of my tumultuous holiday to the surface, even though I've told these L.E.P. officers that my experiences are of a personal nature and I do not enjoy recounting them. I don't think it's too much of an exaggeration to say that I have been scarred for life, and if these incompetent "police officers" weren't so busy laughing at my family's proud surname, perhaps they would have realized that the situation I escaped was a situation most dire, indeed. At least I'll have all the more evidence for the civil suit I've been planning for the last few minutes. We'll see who's smiling when I sue the L.E.P. for all they're worth. It will be Jeffrey Wigglebottom who gets the last laugh, I assure you!

Let me start by explaining a bit about myself. I am an artist first and foremost, a photographer who specializes in capturing the beauty of the fairy condition. I've been known to photograph a pixie in her darkest hour or a troll in a rare moment of self-reflection. My artwork decorates the walls of some of the finest personal residences in all of Haven City. In point of fact, my parents have three of my photos currently hanging on their refrigerator, and that's no small accomplishment, as that space is usually reserved for photos of my younger brother, Jingle Wigglebottom. (How I despise that cherubic buffoon . . .)

As an artiste, I find it insulting that my undiscovered talent must be wasted day in and day out doling out information and snapping lifeless photos of the country yokels who plague the Fountain of Youth. Yes, I understand the Fountain is quite the tourist attraction, and yes, I understand that fairies travel from far and wide to witness the beauty of its magical waters. But you have to understand that after just a week of answering the same questions from obnoxious visitors, you'd be jaded, too.

"Can I touch the water?" they ask.

"No, you may not," I say. "There is a sign posted directly above the Fountain. It says 'Do not touch the water.'"

"Is it warm?" they ask.

"I don't know," I say. "I am also not permitted to touch the water."

"Can I drink it?" they ask.

"If you're not permitted to touch the water, what makes you think you may possibly drink it?"

"Right, right," they say. "But maybe if I just touch it real quick..."

And then I have to have another group of tourists escorted from the premises by force. It's all so tiring, especially when my job is simply to take a quick photo for these unsophisticated ruffians to purchase from my employers for an exorbitant amount of money.

This guy sure does tend to drone on, doesn't he?

—Captain Holly Short

Right, then. Now where was I?

Oh yes, my holiday.

As a hardworking gnome sick to death of country bumpkins crowding my personal space, I wanted to get as far away as possible. So when my holiday time came around, I didn't even consider visiting a popular fairy destination like

Tara or the Bermuda Triangle. I chose to utilize a chute from Haven City that hadn't been used for ages. I decided to use chute E19 and head to the middle of nowhere, Ohio.

If you've never been to the United States of America, then you probably don't know much about the place the Mud People have designated as Ohio. It's about as American as America gets, full of empty bean fields, winding country roads, and something unexplainable known as big-box stores. (They look nothing like boxes, so their naming is quite lost on me.) While Ohio might seem rather boring to the average gnome, to me it sounded like the most wonderful place in the world. Just imagine: you can walk for miles and not see a single human being or fairy. Absolute, solitary bliss.

So I took the chute to Casstown, Ohio, and while it was a bit of a bumpy ride because of the numerous spiderwebs blocking the tunnel, I popped up topside just in time to be greeted by a beautiful full moon.

Now, my magic levels were already rather high, so this wasn't the type of holiday that required the Ritual. In fact, I'd recharged just a year or two prior when I visited Scotland for my cousin's wedding. So there I was, beautiful moon above and not another face to be seen anywhere in the immediate vicinity. The chute emptied out into a pasture of sorts. I couldn't even detect a road nearby. But I didn't mind the walk. The solitude was the reason I'd gone there in the first place.

However, that's when the universe began to conspire against me. In hindsight, it might have been a good idea to find a nice tree for shelter when I felt the first raindrop on my nose. But in my defense, I was excited to be away from it all. A little summer shower didn't frighten me. Quite the contrary. I found it invigorating! So I kept on walking, and the sky kept on raining.

About a half hour into my journey, I realized that this was not the lovely summer shower I had hoped it to be. The moon had all but disappeared in the sky because of the rather aggressive rain clouds. I was finding it hard to see my nose in front of my face, and as you might have noticed, we Wigglebottoms have rather impressive snouts. Not to brag, but I've been told that when I go swimming and perform the backstroke, I give the impression that a shark is in the vicinity.

So there I was, walking through an ever-muddying pasture, just trying to place one foot in front of the other. It was then that I collided with a nightmare creature, a beast so frightening I find I lack the words to describe it sufficiently.

While it was very dark, I could tell the monster was both white and black, undoubtedly camouflaged to match some hideous and unimaginable landscape. It had a pink under-belly (I know, because I was quite under its belly at the time) with strange protrusions sticking out. Perhaps they were spikes, perhaps not. But they looked terrifying!

And no sooner was I out from under its four massive and powerful legs than it detected me. It craned its neck down toward me and opened its terrifying maw.

"Mooo!" it exclaimed in some American dialect I'd never encountered in all my many travels. "Mooo!" it yelled again.

I had no choice. What else could I do? I gathered all my strength, all my inner courage, and I ran. I ran as fast as my gnome legs could carry me. Sure, I slipped a few times on the wet grass, but that should not discount my bravery. I was an impressive specimen that night, I assure you!

I mean, we're all aware he's talking about a cow, right? Big, friendly things that don't do much. Stand around eating their cud and all that? I mean, good for you, wigglebottom, facing a cow!

—HS

Through the raging wind and rain, I soldiered on. By the time I reached a human dwelling, I was thoroughly soaked. I was certainly not in my right mind. I was beset with fear. My heart pounded faster than the wings of a sprite late for a sale at the candy store. I was filled with such absolute dread that when I spied the old farmhouse, I felt that I had no recourse but to make use of its shelter.

It is quite against fairy laws to enter the dwelling of a Mud Person without consent. Despite my terrified condition, I was still aware of that fact. I had been a loyal rule follower my entire life, and I was not about to start breaking the law now. But there is nothing in *The Booke of the People* that states that hiding on the back porch of a quiet home is forbidden. If there had been a STAY OFF sign or perhaps a NO SOLICITING notification, then I would have had to think twice about my decision. But on that particular night, in that particular state of mind, I was willing to take whatever liberty I could properly justify.

So I rounded the farmhouse with all the haste I could muster. I made my way past a soggy garden and located the residence's back porch. It was a lovely sight, all things considered. The porch not only was protected from the rain, but it also contained a cozy chair with nice large armrests. When I snuggled on its plush cushion, the armrests blocked the biting wind. It was absolutely perfect. I could sit there and stay dry and warm until the storm let up and the moon shone its brilliance once more. The beast in the field would not dare tread that close to a human residence. I was finally safe.

Now, I'm not sure how you react when you are completely and utterly warm and safe, but I tend to become a bit drowsy. The exhaustion from my harrowing experience finally caught up with me, and sooner than I would have thought possible, I found myself very much asleep. While that in and of itself was not a problem, the fact that I slept so soundly and on through the next day's sunrise certainly was. In fact, I did not even stir until I heard the house's back screen door creak.

My eyes shot open. My pulse increased once more. But I remained still, lying there on the chair as stiff as a board. And then I saw the face of something far scarier than the beast of the field. I saw a Mud Person.

And still worse: the Mud Person saw me.

She looked to be late in her life. I'd guess she was in her eight hundreds or nine hundreds at the least. She was not enhanced with the youth of fairy magic, so it was quite difficult to form an accurate estimate. She had gray curly hair and eyeglasses that covered the majority of her face, giving her the appearance of a wise old owl, albeit one with significantly few feathers.

"Well, hello there," the Mud Woman said to me.

I remained frozen in place. Was it too late to use magic

to conceal myself? I believed so. Finding a gnome on one's porch was one thing. Finding it and then watching it vanish into the ether was another thing altogether.

Then the Mud Woman bellowed. "Jack! Jack, did you buy a gnome?" she shouted at some unseen Jack, presumably inside the dwelling.

While I kept myself from reacting, I was appalled. Did Mud People actually buy and sell gnomes as if we were mere possessions? The surface world held more disgusting surprises than I'd realized.

"What?" came a voice that had seemingly been used too much in its time.

"A gnome!" shouted the Mud Woman. "Did you buy a gnome?"

"What?" The voice sounded less patient now. Frankly, it had never seemed that patient in the first place.

"A gnome, Jack!"

"I *am* home!"

The elderly Mud Woman sighed and then looked down at me once again.

"Well, we'll need to find a place for you," she said.

I didn't answer. I believe I was in shock, as my body refused to move even the slightest muscle. I don't think I even blinked, if I'm remembering the situation correctly.

The Mud Woman reached down with both hands and picked me up. I couldn't believe the audacity! We weren't even on a first-name basis!

"Oof," she said. "You're a heavy one. They're making you things pretty solid these days."

Solid? I guess I should have been flattered. However, the fact that she was calling me a thing negated any goodwill the compliment might have created. I had no choice but to stay frozen and ride out this accursed wave of strangeness.

Huffing and puffing the whole way (she nevertheless seemed quite in shape for someone quickly approaching a thousand years old), the Mud Woman carried me into her garden. The rain from the previous night had mostly been dried away by the hot sun of the morning. I was just noticing the humidity when the Mud Woman plunked me down—and rather carelessly, at that—right at the far end of her garden. She then gripped me by my shoulders and twisted me back and forth so that I burrowed into the earth a few inches. It was murder on my shiny new loafers. And to think I had purchased them just for that holiday!

"Not too shabby," she said, examining me with her hand under her chin. "The detail is remarkable. I hope Jack didn't spend too much."

And with that peculiar comment, she spun on her heels

with renewed enthusiasm and walked back inside, humming some Mud Person song. As soon as she was out of sight, I tried to lift my feet. My body had recovered from its initial shock, and I thought it best not to wait around in bright daylight any longer. If I was going to escape this mad Mud Woman's clutches, it was now or never!

Then I saw it. Standing there, at the opposite corner of the garden, was a gnome nearly my height. He wore a pointed cap, and it seemed obvious from first glance that he was a country sort. I sighed audibly. My first contact with a fairy on the surface world, and he was of the exact ilk I had fled Haven City to avoid. I tried my legs again, but the dirt was proving a tougher adversary than I had imagined. I could not raise my new loafers—not even a millimeter. I had no choice but to actually speak to this country bumpkin.

"Um, pardon me," I said.

My fellow gnome did not reply.

"I'm sorry to trouble you, but I think I might be stuck," I said.

The country gnome continued to stare straight ahead, unmoving. He did not react. He did not reply. He was as rude as those fairies at the Fountain of Youth who thought that just because I worked there, they could treat me like some lower life-form. While I admit I had originally stereotyped this country fellow, at least I had been accurate.

"You realize it is quite impolite to ignore a fellow fairy, especially one in trouble," I said. "While you may be happy in this simple life as a lawn ornament for a Mud Person, I, in fact, am an artist. I have a career to return to, thank you very much."

When he didn't respond a third time, I decided I had no other choice but to take action. I summoned all my strength, just as I had when I faced down that black-and-white beast in the meadow. And channeling a power that would make a troll jealous, I ripped one of my feet free from the dirt. True,

So let me get this straight. First this guy has no idea what a cow is, and then he spends the morning talking to a plastic lawn ornament? Not the sharpest cap in the gnome hattery, if you ask me. I see what you are trying to do here, Root, show recruits what can happen if they don't follow rules . . . but I really hope none of them are as dense as this gnome, or else we have a lot more to worry about.

—Captain Holly Short

the earth stole my new shoe, but I didn't care. I was fueled by adrenaline. Nothing mattered except my freedom!

My other foot followed suit. However, this foot was not only freed of its dirt prison and shoe; it also somehow lost its sock. With one foot bare and one foot stocking-clad, I ran as fast as I could back the way I had come.

It took what seemed like ages. I could have been running for months for all I knew. But I finally arrived back at the chute. The vicious beast of the field had fled by then, so it presented no obstacle. Obviously it either had heard rumor of my heroic escape or had witnessed my feat of strength. Whatever the case, my return trip was a hardship, yes, but I did not have to battle any foes along the way.

The rest of the journey you can easily imagine. I strapped back into my titanium pod and plotted a return course to Haven City. Shoeless and without holiday, I went home to clean up. But before I could even take a refreshing shower, you L.E.P. meddlers arrived on my doorstep.

"Jeffrey Wigglebottom," said the L.E.P. officer at my door. After a good five minutes of laughing at my name, he finally continued. "You are under arrest for failure to disguise oneself when in the presence of a human being. In addition, you are charged with leaving evidence of fairydom—namely a sock and two overpriced loafers—on the surface."

After that, the officer read me my rights, and before I knew it, here I was. Incarcerated. Me, a highly talented artist. A beautiful voice of the People. A bright light in the eternal twilight of Haven City.

Well, I plan to be out of this place in no time flat, believe you me. My lawyer, one Phineas Stinkybum (and yes, he's heard all your jokes, too), tells me that since I was disguising myself as a decorative lawn ornament, these charges are without merit. While I admit I have no idea what he's talking about, I will say that I agree with him wholeheartedly. My presence on the surface in no way endangered fairy-kind. If anything, charges should be brought upon that unhelpful gnome in the Mud Woman's yard.

And that's all I have to say about that.

That's all? Really? The Mud People have a saying: "Brevity is the soul of wit." Now I finally understand what it means.

Thanks for that, Root. That is a good half hour I'll never get back. I see what you are trying to do but might suggest we simplify. . . . Again, just a thought.

—Captain Holly Short

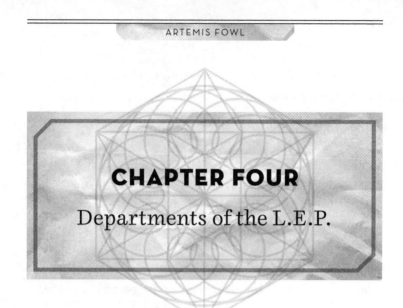

CHAPTER FOUR

Departments of the L.E.P.

The Lower Elements Police is made up of dozens of departments, but the two most important are Recon and Retrieval. To the Mud People living aboveground, Recon is undoubtedly more famous. So that's where we'll begin.

L.E.P.RECON

L.E.P.recon, or Recon for short, ironically enough inspired humans to develop the term "leprechaun." Humans have long included fairies in their legends;

however, they remain ignorant of the different classifications of the People. Those few remaining surface dwellers who believe in magical creatures are still under the mistaken notion that "leprechaun" is a race rather than simply a job description. But again, these are Mud People we're talking about here. They're more known for their destruction of the Earth with their pollutants and obnoxious media than for their razor-sharp brains.

L.E.P. BADGE

Recon is half of police work. It is, simply put, to locate and observe. Recon officers are experts at blending into their environment. They never let themselves be spotted by human beings in any situation. Recon officers have to master flying with police-issued wings, learn how to use their magic to sufficiently shield themselves from possible onlooking Mud People, and learn how to speak and understand a variety of languages the humans utilize (because Mud People can't

HOW TO TELL A MUD PERSON FROM A FAIRY

◉ Is the subject **TALL**? While some Mud People can be rather short, being tall is a dead giveaway. Anyone over four feet merits special caution.

◉ Does the subject say things like **"SOCIAL MEDIA"** and/ or **"SELFIE"**? These are human terms and could very well mean you're in the presence of a Mud Person.

◉ Is the subject wearing **SANDALS WITH SOCKS**? Only Mud People do this. Run away quickly!

even be bothered to agree on a common way to speak to one another).

A L.E.P. recon officer's job is to seek out their target—whether that be a goblin who has escaped Howler's or simply fairy vacationers venturing too close to Disney World—and observe the subject's location and situation. The L.E.P. recon then reports their findings to L.E.P. Central Command and allows their commanding officers to decide whether the situation is a false alarm or one that requires the direct intervention of a Retrieval Extraction Team.

Go, Recon! Or should I say, go, us! Glad you started with what is clearly the most important department.

—HS

L.E.P. RETRIEVAL

Don't ask me why this name didn't catch on with the humans as well, but for one reason or another, it just didn't stick in the minds of the Mud People. Retrieval is our action team. These are the fearless officers charged with the tasks of confronting fairy folk running amok, stopping humans who get too close to fairy truths, and, in some cases, removing the evidence of fairies who ventured to the surface world.

It should be noted that I strongly believe fairies should never journey topside at all. But unfortunately, so many things are not up to me. Besides our civilians wanting to vacation in the "fresh" air of the world above, we all know that fairies must journey to the surface to perform the Ritual from time to time to replenish our magic. The surface is a necessary evil, despite its being infested with more humans than you can shake a wand at.

Those who choose or are pulled out of the academy to be part of L.E.P. Retrieval are some of our brightest officers. They need to be knowledgeable in holographic projection and mind-wipe technology. They need to be experts in working together, from making V-shaped flight patterns, like geese, to hunting their prey in a pack, like wolves. These

REQUIRED L.E.P.
MARTIAL ARTS

- ◉ **KARATE**
- ◉ **TAE GNOME DO**
- ◉ **KUNG FU**
- ◉ **HAND-TO-HAND COMBAT**

Hey, how come the Retrieval guys get to take those nice cushy shuttles while Recon gets stuck rocketing topside in pods? Also, do they get paid more? And one more thing—brightest? Really? Did you need to put that in there? These guys have big enough heads as it is!

—Captain Holly Short

are our toughest soldiers, equipped in fighting and the strategic arts of combat.

Only the best and brightest of the L.E.P. make it into Retrieval. But don't let that intimidate you. Let that inspire you. All officers in the Lower Elements Police should push themselves to the edge of their comfort zone and beyond. To achieve greatness in our ranks, you need to strive for the impossible in any given situation.

The best of those best might find themselves working as L.E.P. Retrieval One commandos. Retrieval One is as elite as it gets. The commandos perform missions with the precision of surgeons. If you become one of the twelve who wear the black jumpsuit of Retrieval One, congratulations: you've made it to the head of the class. Just don't let that head get swollen. I've lost more than one honorable soldier to a chronic case of inflated ego.

Again with the best and brightest. Can we not make L.E.P. Retrieval seem quite so . . . amazing? Half those cowboys are more interested in busting down doors than busting perps. We should be trying to get new recruits to go into Recon—where the brains and action are!

—HS

UNIFORMS

Getting back to human misconceptions (of which we know there are many), we've seen that the look of L.E.P.recon and L.E.P. Retrieval officers has been quite misconstrued in the Mud People world. While it's true that our Recon officers used to wear rather, well, goofy green suits, knickerbockers, and large buckles on their boots and top hats, those uniforms have been retired for at least a century now. But peek into any human school classroom or greeting card store around Saint Patrick's Day and you'll see nothing but offensive caricatures of

L.E.P. UNIFORMS

our people wearing those garish and outdated uniforms. I don't need to say it, but I will: it is obviously just another example of Mud People's brains being a bit, well, muddy.

No, today L.E.P. Recon and Retrieval dress for the job at hand. We utilize formfitting uniforms that allow for range of movement during operations. Our suits are equipped with thermal coils for heating in colder climates. They even have reinforced ribbing to help protect the wearer from physical harm when combat is unavoidable.

Also available for special missions are our state-of-the-art blackout suits. These skintight uniforms are built to protect a fairy from radiation or the threat of radiation. They come complete with a gauge to detect any dips in pressure that could indicate a rip in the suit itself. We don't take any chances with our officers. After all, lawsuits are expensive, and who has that kind of budget?

Just another suggestion to maybe be a little, um, softer here. Maybe downplay the whole budget thing and say something about us—I mean, officers—being invaluable. Importance of protecting life . . . or something.

Again, please don't fire me!

—HS

THE FAIRY COUNCIL

Despite what the Mud People would have you believe, the L.E.P. is not a whimsical organization. These are the toughest men and women in the Underground. But no system should be without its checks and balances—meaning even the L.E.P. has a ruling body to report to. (So if you have an issue with the suits, take it up with, well, the suits.)

That ruling body is the *Fairy Council*.

While I've certainly been accused of running the Lower Elements Police any way I wish, the truth of the matter is that even I must answer to the Fairy Council. The seven fairies who make up this elected body are in place to ensure that *The Booke of the People* is followed to a T. They're in place to make sure the L.E.P. is following the laws of the land and not just governing the People however we see fit. As many times as I've been irritated by the red tape we at the L.E.P. often have to wade through, I

I bet you wouldn't protest if they decided to give you a little wiggle room now and again....

—HS

will admit I'm glad that there's a system in place to make sure no one takes on too much power or responsibility.

While many civilians and L.E.P. officers have their eyes on a position in the council, I certainly have no intentions of ever entering the political arena. I'd rather keep my head down and get my job done than try to please everybody at the same time, which politicians are known to do. That means I've clashed with the Fairy Council from time to time, but never without good reason. Sometimes you have to fight for what's right, even if that means getting the boss angry.

But that doesn't apply to me, got it? If I'm not an altogether perfect boss and commander, I'm darn well close.

You might want to reread that last sentence. Highlight it if you need to. *Just don't forget it.*

No comment.

—Captain Holly Short

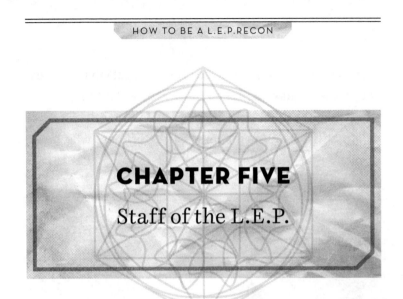

CHAPTER FIVE

Staff of the L.E.P.

The Lower Elements Police is an ancient institution, especially when compared to the civilization of the short-lived Mud People who populate the surface. Our organization attempts to be as accommodating to new recruits as possible, but as in any field, longevity matters. Working for the L.E.P. is a lifelong commitment and one that shouldn't be entered into lightly. We do a dangerous job and put our lives on the line for the sake of the Underground and the surface world. And we do it daily.

This kind of work has a way of weeding out the true

fairies from the faint of heart. If you've got what it takes, you'll always have a place in our ranks. And to give you a better idea of what that prized stuff is exactly, it seems best just to let you meet some of the officers who make up our police force.

L.E.P. PERSONNEL RECORD

CONFIDENTIAL

Commander Root

Elf

TELL US, IN AS MUCH OR AS LITTLE DETAIL AS YOU FEEL NECESSARY, ABOUT YOURSELF AND YOUR ROLE IN THE L.E.P.

Okay, I'll get things started off correctly. You know me as Commander Root, and while I've lost count of exactly how many years I've been with the L.E.P., it is at least seven hundred. (Elves work notoriously hard and for notoriously long stretches of time. We do not enjoy "downtime," as the Mud People call it.)

As the commander at the Lower Elements Police, I do most of my day-to-day work inside headquarters. That's not to say I don't get to the surface every now and again. I'm a hands-on type, even if the Fairy Council wishes otherwise. As soon as they save the whole blasted world from goblin gang wars and troll rampages, I'll start listening to their opinions on police procedure. Until then, I'll keep doing what I've been doing as it seems to have been working, thank you very much.

The big takeaway here is that I'm in charge. Listen to commands, go by the book (both the *Booke* and this book), and you and I will get along just fine.

Now if you'll excuse me, I've got better things to do than write a tell-all exposé about my feelings. You want touchy-feely stuff like that, try talking to someone like Captain Short.

Hey! I resent That.

But if you really want me to talk about my feelings, I'm certainly feeling something right now that I wouldn't mind sharing. . . .

—HS

COMMANDER
ROOT

L.E.P. PERSONNEL
RECORD
CONFIDENTIAL

Captain Holly Short

Elf

TELL US, IN AS MUCH OR AS LITTLE DETAIL AS YOU FEEL NECESSARY, ABOUT YOURSELF AND YOUR ROLE IN THE L.E.P.

I'm not sure exactly what you want me to say. I mean, this instruction is pretty vague. Was that intentional? Did Commander Root make this form herself, because if so, that explains a lot. Wait, is she going to read this? Don't print this section, okay? Can I start over?

Hi, I'm *Captain* Holly Short. I'm still not used to the "captain" part. It looks so weird when I write it down. Good weird, of course. But weird just the same.

So, yeah, I'm an elf. Hence the pointy ears. But I guess

you want me to talk about my job? I work in Recon, and I'm pretty darn good at it, if I'm being honest.

But it took work to get here. Despite my being a whole meter tall and coming from an impressive line of fairies—my great-grandfather was Cupid, for Keebler's sake!—my father's reputation kept some doors closed at first. But I've proven time and again that I'm trustworthy—and capable.

I'm not saying I'm perfect, though. I mean, who is? When I first started out, I made a tiny mistake that seemed to haunt me in everything I did afterward. Okay, the Hamburg Affair wasn't so much a tiny mistake as it was a colossal screwup of titanic proportions. But how can I be blamed when my perp was the one who skipped to the surface and tried to make deals with the Mud People? That's on him. Let's not even dwell on it any further, all right? And I mean, we *could* look at it as some great training for what happened later. Getting all those officers organized and topside? Pretty impressive maneuvering by our fearless commander.

Anyway, after the Hamburg thing (no dwelling, remember?), I had ten successful recon missions without error. And then, I met Artemis Fowl.

Sadly, that seems to be the thing

See that, Root? Even before the whole promotion thing, I was your biggest fan!

—HS

CAPTAIN

HOLLY SHORT

most fairies know about me: my first adventure with that . . . less-than-savory human boy. But everything worked out in the end (or sort of worked out, at any rate), and without my dealings with those Mud People, I wouldn't be here, with a shiny new "Captain" in front of my name.

So, is that enough? I mean, is that the sort of thing you guys want me to write down? Feel free to cut out the part about Hamburg. I have no idea why I mentioned it. Also, don't print this part, either, okay? What is this even for again?

Seriously? I thought they were going to edit that stuff out! You left that in there on purpose, Root!

—HS

L.E.P. PERSONNEL RECORD

CONFIDENTIAL

Chief Technical Officer
Foaly, Centaur

TELL US, IN AS MUCH OR AS LITTLE DETAIL AS YOU FEEL NECESSARY, ABOUT YOURSELF AND YOUR ROLE IN THE L.E.P.

Hello, then. I'm Officer Foaly, and you might say I'm the brains behind this operation. You might say it because it's accurate. And I might say it because I've never been one for modesty. Just a waste of time, if you ask me.

I'm a centaur, and as you are probably aware, there aren't too many of us these days. But I don't judge myself solely on my background and my fairy type. I judge myself on my mind, and it's a brilliant blob of gray matter, that's for sure.

My job? Well, it's a big one. And an important one. Which makes sense, as only someone with my brains could do it. You see, I'm not just in charge of making sure all the L.E.P. equipment runs like clockwork; I'm the clockmaker himself. I've got more patents than any other fairy in history. All of history, mind you. That includes ancient history, modern history— you name it!

Over the course of my career, I've figured out how to stop time. I've streamlined

I say let Foaly brag as much as he wants. Sure, he's a little kooky, but the L.E.P. wouldn't be near as efficient without him. He's our resident four-legged genius.

—HS

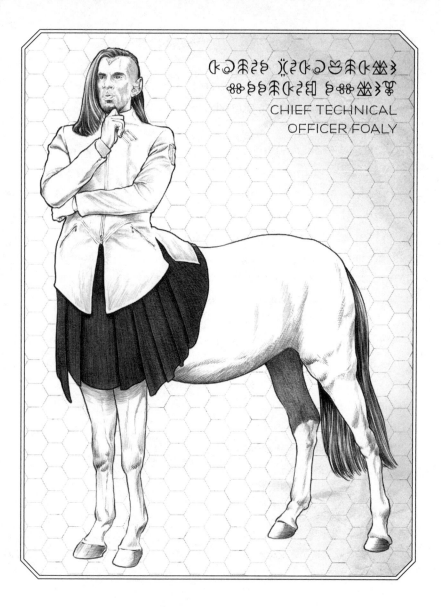

CHIEF TECHNICAL
OFFICER FOALY

equipment to get us out of the dark ages, and I've helped piggyback relays on man-made satellites, giving the L.E.P. unprecedented access to views aboveground. That's just the tip of the iceberg, but I've been told I have a tendency to prattle on a bit. Some fairies even have the nerve to say I've got an overactive ego. Can you believe that?

I think it's just my sense of humor that has them rattled. But life's too short not to laugh once in a while, I always say. A thousand years can speed by as fast as the titanium chute pods I designed. Oh, am I being immodest again? Ah, well, let's let history decide all that, shall we? (Oh, that. I also write the history books, you see.)

L.E.P. PERSONNEL
RECORD

CONFIDENTIAL

Major Briar Cudgeon

Elf

TELL US, IN AS MUCH OR AS LITTLE DETAIL AS YOU FEEL NECESSARY, ABOUT YOURSELF AND YOUR ROLE IN THE L.E.P.

I am, in fact, Major Briar Cudgeon. Of course, if I had my way, an elf of my stature—thirty-four inches, mind you—would be in a much higher position of authority than mere major. The fact of the matter is I *have* been in a higher position from time to time. But for the purposes of this rudimentary exercise, I'll just use the rank major, no matter my feelings on the subject. It takes a big elf not to bother with political rankings and to simply do his job. And again, I'm thirty-four inches tall. No, really, you can measure me. Well, no, not right now. As it turns out, I'm very busy.

I honestly have no idea why I've been asked to fill out this form. Seems like a waste of police time and money. But I'm so rarely asked when it comes to important matters. The blame for that falls right at the feet of Commander Root, of course. If those of you reading this had any sense, you would ask her why I haven't raced up the ranks of the L.E.P. My résumé is certainly more than impressive, as are my connections to the Fairy Council. Why I haven't been inducted into that particular political body is beyond me.

As a major in the Lower Elements Police, I have the official assignment of commanding the Retrieval squad.

MAJOR BRIAR
CUDGEON

Unofficially, I find it advantageous to monitor Commander Root's actions and statements and to keep a watchful eye on her loyal lapdogs, like that insolent officer Foaly. That one thinks he's so clever. Problem with all centaurs, if you ask me.

It is my firm belief that if we don't police our own, well, police, then we're doomed to serve out the whims of impulsive leaders. And I, for one, don't plan on being sent marching to my grave or, even worse, being made to work with Mud People from the surface.

My first duty is to fairy-kind. No, scratch that. My first duty is to myself. Because if one can't be true to one's own beliefs, then one isn't much of a fairy, now, is one?

Any other road leads to folly. Or, just as accurately, Foaly. I mentioned that I hate that centaur, didn't I?

I couldn't make it past his first sentence. Did Cudgeon invent the yawn? I'm going to take a wild leap here and say I didn't miss anything important.

—HS

L.E.P. PERSONNEL
RECORD
CONFIDENTIAL

Corporal Trouble Kelp
Elf

**TELL US, IN AS MUCH OR AS LITTLE DETAIL AS YOU FEEL
NECESSARY, ABOUT YOURSELF AND YOUR ROLE IN THE L.E.P.**

Trouble Kelp here, and if you notice my name, you already know what I stand for. Sure, I gave myself the first name Trouble, but that doesn't make it any less accurate.

I work for Retrieval. Specifically, L.E.P. Retrieval One. Yes, those commandos. I know, I know. But I don't let the fame and prestige get in my way. I have a job to do. And I do it to the best of my abilities. The same can't exactly be said about my brother, Grub. But the less said about him, the better.

Not only am I a member of L.E.P. Retrieval One, I'm squad

⦗⟨✦✦⟩⦘⟨✦✦⟩⟨✦✦⟩
⟩⟨⟨✦✦⟩⟨⟩
⟨⟩⟨⟩

CORPORAL
TROUBLE KELP

I'll say that for Trouble: he
does take his job quite
seriously. If I was in the
thick of it, I wouldn't mind
having him on my team. Of
course, he could afford to
loosen up just a smidge....

—HS

leader. I call the shots. I make the hard decisions. I charge my
men into the fray, and I rarely back down until the battle's won.
L.E.P. Retrieval is the fairy world's defense against human

interference, troll attacks, goblin violence, and dwarf home invasions. My officers' abilities and accuracy are the result of years of hard work and discipline, and I'm darn proud of every last one of them. Again, except for Grub.

What I'm trying to say is that I take my job very seriously. If you're working for me, you will, too.

L.E.P. PERSONNEL
RECORD
CONFIDENTIAL

Private Grub Kelp
Elf

TELL US, IN AS MUCH OR AS LITTLE DETAIL AS YOU FEEL NECESSARY, ABOUT YOURSELF AND YOUR ROLE IN THE L.E.P.

So you want to know about me? Okay, well, the first thing you need to know is that I don't take my job all that seriously. (Obviously, or I wouldn't be writing this down!) It's just a gig, you know what I mean? Sure, the benefits are nice and you've got plenty of adventure and excitement built right into your schedule, but some days I think I'd be happier selling snail-trail paintings or, I don't know, working in IT or HR or another pair of letters that describe a job I don't understand.

Mommy says she's proud of her rough-and-tumble boys, so it's hard to actually commit to a career change at this point in my life. Especially when you've got a brother like Trouble, who makes everything a competition. "Stop falling asleep, Grub," he says. "Keep your safety on, Grub." "Don't accidentally bump into that troll, Grub." Who has time to remember that many rules?

PR! That's another one of those two-letter jobs. Just thought of it now.

I really gotta look up what those mean.

Well, I guess you have to admire his honesty.

—HS

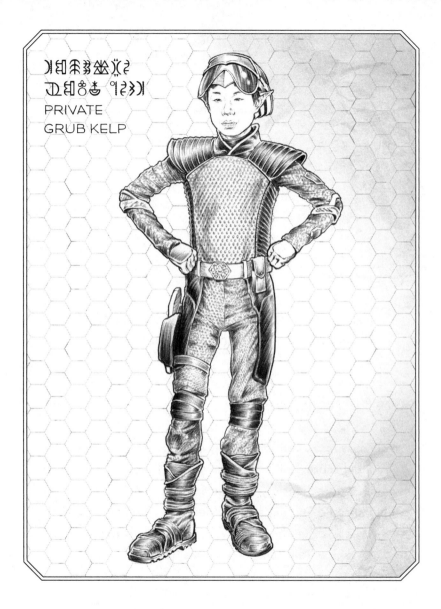

PRIVATE
GRUB KELP

L.E.P. PERSONNEL
RECORD

CONFIDENTIAL

Chix Verbil,

Sprite

TELL US, IN AS MUCH OR AS LITTLE DETAIL AS YOU FEEL NECESSARY, ABOUT YOURSELF AND YOUR ROLE IN THE L.E.P.

Chix Verbil, reporting for duty. I am an L.E.P. officer and one fine-looking ladies' sprite (if I do say so myself). I don't want to hear any more of those slurs about me being an elf. It's a misrepresentation, and I won't stand for it! My father was an elf, sure. But that doesn't mean I'm one. My mother was a sprite, so legally that makes me a sprite. I'd appreciate it if you could tell that to the other guys at the station. They keep razzing me about it. I mean, I'm not so thin-skinned I can't take a little teasing, but this has been going on for years. I'm a sprite, D'Arvit!

CHIX VERBIL

I'd write down my thoughts about Chix Verbil, but I can't seem to stop gagging. Check back with me later.

—HS

Okay, sorry about the salty language. But what can I say? I'm a passionate sort. Sometimes my heart is just too big, you know? Hey, as long as I'm writing this, could you put a good word in for me with Holly Short? I'd be lying if I said I wasn't interested in her, and I know she's got to feel that spark, too.

I mean, just check out my picture. It's hard to believe an elf like Holly wouldn't be a sucker for this million-dollar smile. Yeah, she makes fun of me just like all the other officers at work do, but I think she's just trying to mask her true feelings.

Look at my picture again. Right now. See? That is one fine-looking sprite! Am I right?

L.E.P. PERSONNEL RECORD
CONFIDENTIAL

Professor Cumulus
Elf

Doctor Argon
Gnome

TELL US, IN AS MUCH OR AS LITTLE DETAIL AS YOU FEEL NECESSARY, ABOUT YOURSELF AND YOUR ROLE IN THE L.E.P.

P.C. Hello, I'm Professor Cumulus.

D.A. And I'm Doctor Argon.

P.C. I would like it known that I find it quite unprofessional and downright humiliating to share a form with this Dr. Argon.

D.A. While I rarely agree with my "distinguished" colleague, I will have to agree with him on this point.

P.C. Why did you write "distinguished" in quotes? Was that a jab?

D.A. I thought you were supposed to be a behavioral specialist. Why don't you tell me?

P.C. Oh, that's rich, coming from a staff "psychologist" like yourself.

D.A. Don't think I don't see your quotes as well!

P.C. You started it!

D.A. Did not!

P.C. It's right there. You can read it clear as day!

D.A. Like I'm to believe anything you write.

PROFESSOR CUMULUS

DOCTOR ARGON

P.C. You're impossible, you know that?

D.A. Takes one to know one.

P.C. This is why the L.E.P. can never get a fair assessment of the mental state of its enemies. Your lack of profession- alism is astounding!

D.A. Oh, is that your "professional" opinion?

P.C. Stop using quotes!

D.A. "Fine."

P.C. You're a child, you know that? But what did I expect from an American fairy? You do come from below the United States, after all.

D.A. That's it!

P.C. Stop hitting me! I'm trying to write!

D.A. Never!

Well, that was useful. If I were you, Commander, I'd consider omitting these two "doctors" from the manual completely. (See? I can use quotes, too!)

—HS

FREELANCE AGENTS

Root here again. I just need to break in and make a few quick but important notes before we go on to the last few members of our "staff."

First, on behalf of the L.E.P., I'd like to apologize for the candid language used by some of my officers. As I said earlier, we're in desperate need of new blood here at the Lower Elements Police. Some of my staff have grown complacent and could use a swift kick in the unmentionables, if you'll excuse my mentioning them.

Second, for that reason, and a few others, the L.E.P. occasionally employs freelance agents. These temporary allies are often selected for possessing an outstanding skill set, one that can be specifically exploited to accomplish a specialized task. Obviously, freelancers aren't the ideal choice, as many of them have criminal records. But with a corrupt history comes the ability to go where law-abiding citizens can't, the ability to break into homes or office buildings that would cause honest magic users to become violently ill from the backlash or lose their powers altogether.

Um, just a suggestion here—and of course, your book, so your call— but maybe lay off words like "desperate" and "corrupt" in an official police manual?

—HS

I will always explore every avenue before I let anything happen to the People. If that means cutting deals with some of society's deplorables, then I'll do what I have to do. The protection of fairy-kind is the ultimate goal at the L.E.P., no matter the cost.

L.E.P. PERSONNEL
RECORD

CONFIDENTIAL

Mulch Diggums
Dwarf

TELL US, IN AS MUCH OR AS LITTLE DETAIL AS YOU FEEL NECESSARY, ABOUT YOURSELF AND YOUR ROLE IN THE L.E.P.

I'm an artist. And I'm innocent. I just want those two facts stated for the record. True, I don't know exactly why you're having me write this. But I have been tricked

MULCH
DIGGUMS

before, and I just feel it is important that all parties know I didn't do it.

On the off chance that this isn't some trap set by Commander Root, I guess I'll go ahead and answer. After all, I am always happy to talk about my favorite person: me. My name is Mulch Diggums. I'm a proud dwarf. Is there any other kind? I am also a pretty sweet artist and am working on getting my first solo show based on some work I did while wrongly incarcerated in Howler's. I'm also one of the top diggers in the world—above and below the surface. My jaw can unhinge as quick as the best of them, and I can tunnel as fast as a mole that accidentally dug through a habanero patch.

Now, due to my *alleged* profession as an expert thief, I have acquired special "skills" to relieve individuals of their personal effects one pocket at a time. I've got a real love for aboveground memorabilia. Obviously I enjoy the artwork. I find the impressionists to be quite impressive. But what I like even more than the art is the music. How can you go through life without listening to those singing nuns from that movie? There is more than one kind of magic, and stealing that music has made me a better fairy, I'd wager. All allegedly, of course.

Let's see. What else can I tell you about me? Well, I hate limestone. (It gives me indigestion.) I'm not big on Mud People (especially large bodyguard types), and I am happiest when I'm digging through the dirt, with no cares in the world and the wind whipping through the back flap of my trousers. Other likes? Well, I've got quite a fondness for gold. I'm also entranced by the thrill of the hunt. There's nothing more exciting than breaking into a place you don't belong just to see if you can do it, you know? Nothing like letting your beard hairs slink through a lock to find its tumblers or that satisfying click when you pop open a safe.

But . . . er . . . as I said, I wouldn't know any of that first-hand. Because I'm not a criminal or anything. I'm an innocent little harmless dwarf. The L.E.P. wouldn't have hired me if that wasn't the case, right? Right?

I think I need a lawyer.

Wrong. So, so, sooooo wrong. Root—should we even be including Mulch in here? I mean, it kind of seems like a bad call. But again, your manual, your rules. Just doing what you asked me to do. At least he didn't mention his constant need to ask me out!

—Captain Holly Short

TROLLS

This is rather simple. Trolls are bad news. Very bad news indeed. I cannot stress this enough. Trolls are bad news.

But on occasion—a very rare occasion—the Lower Elements Police has been forced to . . . take the road less traveled. And while I'm very much against this policy, a troll has been called in to do the L.E.P.'s bidding in the past, even without the troll's consent.

Now, I find this sort of thing a fairy-rights violation, not to mention cruel and unusual punishment for the troll (even if they are bad, they have rights) and all those in the troll's way, but that doesn't mean there's not a historical precedent. What I'm talking about here is using a troll to conduct fairy warfare—namely, setting a rampaging troll loose on an unsuspecting target.

If you don't know much about trolls, be sure to peruse the section of this manual on the different varieties of fairy folk. Also, if you don't know much about trolls, that's even more of a reason to stay away from them. They're beasts and behemoths with barely two brain cells to string between the lot of them. I hate to sound speciesist, but these brutes give all of fairy-kind a bad name. There's a reason so many of them live under bridges. The rest of polite society has completely rejected them. Even billy goats.

Anyway, back to the point. The Fairy Council has used a troll or two in the past to cause the kind of

If you're in need of a troll exterminator, look no further than Captain Holly Short. Okay, so I'm more like a troll distractor. But I do come highly recommended!

—Captain Holly Short

uncontrollable damage only a troll can cause. But in my experience, that's like unleashing rats in your apartment to take care of your mouse infestation. Sure, you get rid of the mice, but now you've got an even bigger problem on your hands.

THOSE WE'VE LOST

Obviously there are now, and have been, more members of the Lower Elements Police than I can possibly make room for in this book.

Over the years, we've lost our fair share of valiant men and women, and I'd be remiss if I didn't take this opportunity to thank them for their service. While many have sacrificed their very lives for the L.E.P., others have left our ranks under more ambiguous circumstances.

I'm sure you've all heard the rumors revolving around the disappearance of Captain Birchwood Short. Birchwood was in my direct employ, as I was his team leader, when the unfortunate events surrounding his role within the L.E.P. began. He also happens to be the father of one Holly Short, an individual I'd trust with my life despite her family history.

There is no way of knowing if the controversy surrounding Birchwood Short is legitimate. He was accused of selling magic to the Mud People. That was never proven, but Captain Birchwood disappeared from the Underground soon after the allegations were brought to light.

Rather than using Birchwood's story to besmirch the image of the L.E.P., or Captain Holly Short in particular, I would rather we look at this as a learning opportunity. Birchwood Short should serve as an example of what can happen to an L.E.P. officer's life and reputation if he or she chooses to consort with humans from the surface. The People are *not* to associate with humans, and that goes double for members of the L.E.P. I hope I've made myself clear enough. It really would be a shame to lose another member of my team.

Thank you? I guess. Sort of? Lot going through my mind here . . .

—HS

CHAPTER SIX

Cautionary Tale #2

TALE #2 TAKEAWAY:
A FAIRY MUST
HAVE PERMISSION
TO ENTER A HUMAN'S
DWELLING.

This next real-world lesson comes from a former L.E.P.recon officer, emphasis on the word "former." You'll see why as you dig into his little story.

LOWER ELEMENTS POLICE
OFFICER INCIDENT REPORT

INITIAL REPORT: #256-491-218-19

STATEMENT BY: PLANK, PIDGE

LOCATION: POLICE HEADQUARTERS, HAVEN CITY

I should start by saying that I am an elf. Pidge Plank is the name. Although it could very well be Plank Pidge. My mum can sometimes get mixed up and not know whether she's coming or going. She thinks the family name is Plank, but she also used to think the dog's name was Cat. And of course we don't own either animal. We're elves.

So I suppose you need me to start telling my story. Well, it all began when my commanding officer sent me on an assignment to a mystical place called New Jersey. It sounded much more wonderful than Old Jersey. I was personally very curious about the improvements the state must have made to give it such a modern name. I took my designated chute up to the surface and switched on my shielding. I had 99 percent magic, as I never miss a chance to recharge. Who would?

Anytime I can look up at a full moon, I'm happy. Although I'm also happy anytime I can't. I'm pretty much happy all the time. It really bothers my mum! Sorry, Mum!

When I got to the surface, I was surprised to see so many Mud People. They were all hustling about their day, driving around in their automobiles or on their bicycles. One large truck nearly hit me, but I'm sure I was at fault. It seems he was a busy gentleman and couldn't wait in the heavy street traffic. So he wisely took a shortcut and drove down the sidewalk for a bit. Whatever possessed me to walk along that very sidewalk, I'll never know. I can be so silly sometimes!

Anyway, after I picked myself up from that ditch I'd flung myself into, I remembered I wasn't just in New Jersey to see the many wonderful sights—like that Mud Woman yelling at a store clerk and that little child attached to his parent by a leash. I was there for a top secret L.E.P. mission!

This is the juicy part! You see, there were rumors that a pixie was living in an apartment building in the middle of a wonderful village called Newark. It was a fabulous place full of interesting Mud People. If I hadn't been on assignment, I would have spent hours watching an old man play chess against a pigeon near the train station, but I had a job to do, and darn tootin', I was going to do it!

Using the mapping system built into my flight helmet,

I located the address in question: 224 Avenue B. Avenue B! It's certainly the avenue to *be* on, if you ask this elf. When I got to the address (after a minor collision with a bus stop—they sure do keep that glass clean!), I took a few minutes and marveled at the impressive structure before me. It was a modern miracle of faded stone, foggy windows, and an awning torn in only six or eight places. Someone had even spent some time writing a few words in spray paint on the building's side. The words themselves weren't very polite, but I guess that's artists for you!

Ugh. If this guy were any sweeter, I'd get a cavity. How did he ever get into the L.E.P. in the first place? Riddle me that, Root!

—Captain Holly Short

Eventually, I realized that duty called. (Sorry about using a rude word like "duty"! It won't happen again!) I took a deep breath, steadied my nerves, and flew right through the front door of the apartment building.

That's when everything started to go . . . well, Mum would say "poorly." I don't like that word, as I think it implies that I wasn't having fun. There's never anything not-fun about New Jersey, let me tell you that!

Although if I had to pick my least favorite part, it was

what happened next. My belly started to make fizzy-funny sounds, and all of a sudden, my breakfast decided it was no longer happy to stay in my tum-tum.

Lucky for me, I managed to get my helmet off in time! Now, I know it's against the rules to take off your helmet for any reason while on the surface, but I couldn't see any way around it. So I did what I had to do. I threw my helmet off and stuck my head in the nearest potted plant I could find. In retrospect, it probably wasn't the best idea to throw my helmet out the nearby window, but live and learn, am I right?

He threw up? And this is how he chooses to describe it?

—HS

My tummy troubles didn't seem to want to end, so I stayed near that pot a good thirty minutes. Or it might have been two hours. I was still using my shielding, but that didn't stop a strange little woman from walking right up to me. She grabbed me by my arm (how she could see me, I'll never know!) and pulled me into her apartment.

When the door was slammed behind her, she said, in a not-very-friendly way, "What are you doing here?"

Since my shields weren't doing the job, I stopped using

them. "Hello!" I said. And then I promptly threw up in a pair of her slippers near her front door.

"Stop it!" she shouted. Then she directed me to her bathroom, a welcome sight indeed! "Just wait here," she said in that same very unpleasant tone. I don't like to speak ill of other fairies, but she just seemed so, well, angry.

"Mr. O'Hara," she said into a tiny little phone that could fold and unfold as if by magic! I hear the kids call them flip phones, but I'd never dare to be as hip as today's youth. "I have a guest here in your building," she said into the phone. "Is that okay?"

There was an awkward pause in her conversation then, so I took the opportunity to fill the silence with a dry heave.

"Yes, I know I'm an adult and don't have to tell you about my houseguests. But if you could just say it's okay . . ." she said into the phone. "Yes, I know I'm a very strange lady. Thank you, sir. Have a nice day."

Suddenly, the tummy rumbling stopped altogether.

"Better now?" she said as she glared at me.

Since a glare is altogether better than not being looked at at all, I answered, "Yes!" in the happiest voice I could muster.

Seriously?

—HS

"How do you *not* know the rules by now?" she asked.

"Rules?" I replied.

"You can't enter a human dwelling uninvited. And since I'm a pixie, I can't very well grant you permission to go into a building owned by a Mud Man. I had to call my landlord and sound like a crazy person just to get you to stop throwing up."

"And I'm ever so glad you did!" I said.

"So," she said. She walked to her window and looked out at the courtyard beyond. "You found me."

"I did!" And then I said it again. Because I hadn't realized, really, until just that moment, that I had, in fact, completed my assignment. Well, at least some of it.

"What now?" the pixie asked.

"Well," I said, wondering why I hadn't yet been offered any tea or milk, "I guess I'll have to take you back with me to Haven City. Fairies can't be out and about topside, that's for sure!"

"Huh," she said. She seemed lost in thought. I wish I could have been lost there with her. I bet it was fascinating! "Then shouldn't you make a call to L.E.P. Retrieval?"

"I should do that very thing!" I said. "But I was hoping for some tea and milk first. I've been on the surface for quite some time and have yet to have a snack."

"Oh, where are my manners?" the pixie said. And then

she frowned. It was such a big frown I felt so very sorry for her. "But I don't have any tea."

"Well, then I simply must go to the store and get you some!" I said.

"Oh, you can't go to a human store," she said. "What if you're spotted?"

She had a great point. The only thing to do was return to Haven City, fetch some tea, and then return to her dwelling. After I stated that very plan, the pixie ushered me to her door (quite forcefully, I might add), and we said our goodbyes. I only teared up for a few minutes. Mum would be so proud of what a tough officer I have become.

Well, long story short, I went back to Haven City. I found just the most aromatic Earl Grey after merely a few days of searching, and I returned to lovely Newark to see my new best friend. But after a few hours of tummy issues and exploring random apartments (just in case!), I discovered that the pixie was nowhere to be found. After watching a few rousing man-versus-pigeon chess matches, I returned to Headquarters and told this story with the enthusiasm of an elf half my age.

Then I was fired. While I never understood the reason, I'm sure they had a good one! I'm also sure it all worked out for the best. I didn't want to move out of Mum's house, anyway. And now I not only got to stay put, I also had a full package of tea to show for my adventures. It was quite a mission, or my name isn't Pidge Plank.

And it very well might not be!

I'm not really sure what you are getting at with all these silly stories, Root. I mean, shouldn't fairies accepted into the L.E.P. sort of know better? Although, wait, now I get it. This guy was a fairy and an L.E.P. officer and he certainly didn't get it. Well done, Root. But if you're going to publish this story in the manual, could you maybe at least delete half of those exclamation points? Do it for my sanity, if nothing else.

—HS

CHAPTER SEVEN

Staying in Shape

A big part of being an officer in the Lower Elements Police is staying physically fit. Now this doesn't mean just waking up to do one hundred push-ups and fitting in three dozen jumping jacks on your lunch hour (although those are both requirements and should be checked off your to-do list daily).

This also means keeping on top of your magic. It's essential that a fairy recharges whenever possible. This means that surface trips could be much more frequent if you're on the front lines of duty and you expend heaps and heaps of magical energy on your regular missions. Don't like the Ritual? Don't be a cop. It's that simple.

Again, this feels particularly targeted at me. I could be wrong, but I know you never miss a chance to give a good lecture. Is this the only reason you wanted me to review this book?

—HS

THE RITUAL

The Ritual is a time-honored tradition among fairy folk, and it is certainly every bit as important now as it ever was. While it's true that it's much more difficult nowadays to participate in the Ritual, since fairies live underground, the Ritual still needs to be practiced on a regular basis to ensure an efficient and powerful police force.

For those of you who haven't performed the Ritual in the last few decades, let me break it down for you.

STEP #1: Find an acorn. Find a good one, mind you. The holier the spot the acorn is from, the better. (For a

THE RITUAL

guide to acorn spots throughout the surface, please see "Guides to Getting Magical." This was included in the packet provided by HR upon completion of the hiring process.)

STEP #2: Bury the acorn during a full moon.

STEP #3: Say the oath. Especially the "I return you to the earth and claim the gift that is my right" part. That part is important. If you don't have it memorized, take a few minutes and do that now. But you know what? If you don't have it memorized, I'm beginning to wonder if you should be an officer in the first place.

STEP #4: Sit back and watch your wrist locator's magic reader fill up like a cup left out in a rainstorm. It's just that easy.

This passage from *The Booke of the People* says it best:

⊖ᚾ⚘⚘ᚾ ᚷᚲᚱ ᚱᚥᚥᚾᚱᚲᚺ ᚷᚲᚥ᚜⚘ᚱ ᚷ⚘⚘ᚱᚷᚾ ⊖ᚾ⚘⚘ᚾ᚛

ᚑᚱᚠᚷᚥ ᚷᚲᚺᚾ⚘⚘ᚷᚑᚺ ᚲ⚘⚘ᚺᚾᚷᚷ᚜᚛ᚠ ᚜⚘⚘ ᚷᚺᚥᚥᚠ᚜ ᚥᚾᚺ ⚘⚘ᚷᚱᚷ.

ᚷᚺᚥᚲᚠ ᚷᚺᚾ⚘⚘ᚺ ᚷᚲᚱ ᚥᚥᚑᚱᚲᚠ ᚜ᚱᚱᚷ

ᚠᚥᚷᚺᚱ ⊖ᚺᚱ᚛ ᚥᚷ⚘⚘⚘ᚥ ᚥᚥᚲᚣᚱᚷᚥᚷ ⚘⚘ᚥᚠᚠ ᚥᚥᚥᚷ ᚷᚠᚣᚠᚷᚷᚺ ᚠᚥᚷᚷᚾ ᚥᚠᚣᚷ.

ᚥᚥᚥᚷ ᚣ᚜᚜ᚾ ᚠᚷ ⊖ᚥᚥᚾ ⊖ᚾ⚘⚘ᚾ ᚠᚥᚷᚺᚱ ᚠᚷ ᚠᚥᚠ ⊖⚘⚘ᚺᚥᚷ

᚜⚘⚘ ᚥᚷᚷ᚜ᚣᚥᚷ ᚦ⚘⚘ᚣᚾ ᚑᚠᚠᚲ ᚠᚷᚷ⚘⚘ ᚷᚲᚱ ᚑᚾ⚘⚘ᚣᚥᚷ.

From the earth thine power flows,
Given through courtesy, so thanks are owed.
Pluck thou the magick seed,
Where full moon, ancient oak,
and twisted water meet.
And bury it far from where it was found,
So return your gift into the ground.

Stick to a regular Ritual routine, and you'll be running hot all your days on the force. The last thing we need on the field is an L.E.P. who hasn't recharged in centuries. Keep your magic and your mind primed, and you'll be ready for anything.

Again, really? I get it. I get it. Never let my magic supply get low. Thanks for the loads of not-so-subtle reminders.

—Captain Holly Short

NUTRITION

While the Ritual is a vital part of staying in shape as an L.E.P. officer, feeding one's body is also an important aspect. As much as I'd like to eat at Spud's every day of the week, being in the L.E.P. does mean you have to watch the kind of food you put into your body. Our vending machines are fully stocked with protein and energy bars, crafted specifically with a fairy's dietary needs in mind. And when in doubt, opt for a nettle smoothie in the morning. It will do wonders for your energy levels compared to junk food like deep-fried pit slugs.

A healthy officer is a healthy L.E.P. Remember that.

FITNESS

As previously stated, there is also a rigorous exercise regimen that all members of the L.E.P. are urged to follow. I say "urged," but you know that it is less a request and more a demand. Being in peak physical condition is imperative to being a successful officer. Those goblins are quick, remember? What would happen if you couldn't catch up because you were winded? What if hand-to-hand combat became a necessity and your right uppercut was weak? The answer? Nothing good! On a daily basis, an officer should do *at least* the following:

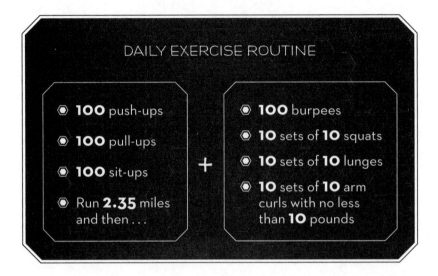

DAILY EXERCISE ROUTINE

◉ **100** push-ups

◉ **100** pull-ups

◉ **100** sit-ups

◉ Run **2.35** miles and then . . .

+

◉ **100** burpees

◉ **10** sets of **10** squats

◉ **10** sets of **10** lunges

◉ **10** sets of **10** arm curls with no less than **10** pounds

At the end of each month, you will be asked to perform this routine in front of your commanding officer to ensure you are making progress.

Um, not trying to be a smart aleck or anything here, but isn't "ten sets of ten" just another way of saying "one hundred"? I mean, your book, your way of saying things . . .

—HS

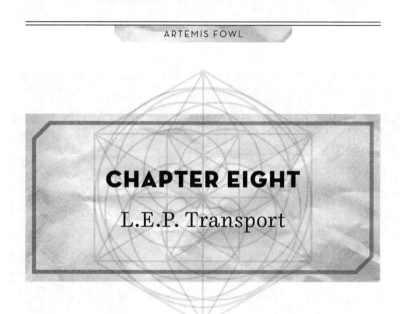

CHAPTER EIGHT

L.E.P. Transport

Hello. Chief Technical Officer Foaly here. Or as I like to refer to myself, Cee-Toff. Okay, I'll be honest and say that I just made that nickname up right here and now. But it's got a nice ring to it, doesn't it?

Anyway, Commander Root has asked me to guide you through all things technical. Which makes sense, as most of the technical things we use here in the L.E.P., I invented. Or patented. Or co-invented. In any case, we are going to start with transportation.

I can see your eyes glazing over already. But trust me, this is the good stuff! Sure, I'm a bit biased, as I—as I've said—designed the majority of it, but don't look a gift centaur in the mouth, right?

Let's get those engines revving!

Oh, this should be fun . . . . I mean, honestly, Root, giving Foaly his own section to write? Like his head isn't big enough already!

—HS

FLY TECH OVERVIEW

Wings seem like a natural enough place to start if we are talking flying tech. Wings are a valued commodity among us fairies, especially if you haven't managed to grow a pair of your own. We centaurs are the land-loving type, but that doesn't mean I don't see how wings are an essential part of crime fighting, both above- and belowground. There's a reason Mud People associate fairies with wings, and I have to say that in the past few decades, I'm pretty much that reason.

(Another fun centaur fact? We can quite easily pat ourselves on the back.)

I've taken the liberty of describing in more detail a few of the wings used by the L.E.P. officers to provide the highest level of protection and safety to the citizens of the Underground. Some of them, of course, I invented.

WING TYPE 1: DRAGONFLIES

Every day I have cadets coming to me with complaints about their wings. The truth of the matter is Dragonflies are clunky. (For the record, I do not want my name associated with these antiquated things. I had no part in their design, only in their implementation.) They're not the least bit aerodynamic, with their double-oval wingspan and their much-too-large motor. I mean, the things still run on a gas engine, for Tara's sake! I've got to admit I cringe when I see an L.E.P. officer struggling with the pull cord to get their Dragonfly started up and their wings flapping. It's just so outdated, not to mention terrible for the environment.

But being in the L.E.P. means making certain compromises. I found this out the hard way when I first glimpsed my rather embarrassing budget. We make do with what we can afford, and at the moment, we can afford Dragonflies. So what if every tween-ager taking a holiday to the surface has better wings than those used by our police force? So what if your Dragonfly might be heavier than a pig dipped in mud? If you're

DRAGONFLY

a good enough pilot, a good enough cop, you'll find a way to do your job with the tools at hand.

No matter how primitive those tools might be.

That's certainly one way to look at it. My take on the upside of wearing a Dragonfly? No one judges you when you treat yourself to a hot lava rock massage after a long day of flying.

—Captain Holly Short

HUMMINGBIRD Z7

Now these little gems are the cream of the crop—the wing pack on everyone's holiday wish list, the best of the best. It's the Hummingbird Z7. These babies are whisper silent and operate on a satellite-bounced solar battery. A single charge could fly a fairy twice around the world if need be. You can get these puppies up to Mach 1 in a pinch (or just for the fun of it). They make flying a breeze, or make it like you're flying on a breeze, depending on your way of thinking. (And, yes, I did invent these beauties!)

But again, budget cuts. So unless you have rich parents or have been saving up your lunch money for a few decades, get used to the smell of your Dragonfly's exhaust. Sorry about that.

FLASH CRUISERS

When you need to fly in style in both the Underground and on the surface, a flash cruiser should do the trick. Wings have a tendency to tire out their hosts, while a cruiser gives you a nice place to park your bum while you let the wonders of fairy technology do the work for you.

These neat little flying vehicles can be launched in even the most congested city. Why, in Haven City you can take off

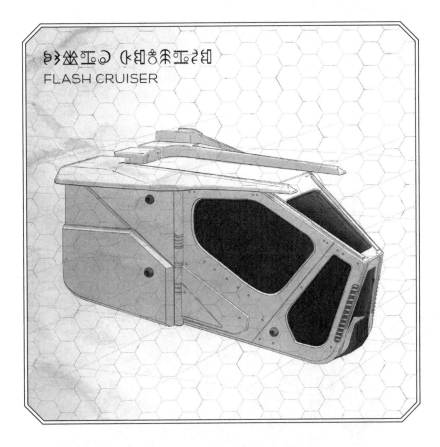

FLASH CRUISER

right from the top of Police Headquarters. They're not for the faint of heart, though. I designed the cruisers to reach a maximum velocity in a minimum time. With power like that under the hood, don't be surprised if you wind up making some barrel rolls or loop the loops just to show off to the rest of the squad.

FLASH CRUISER

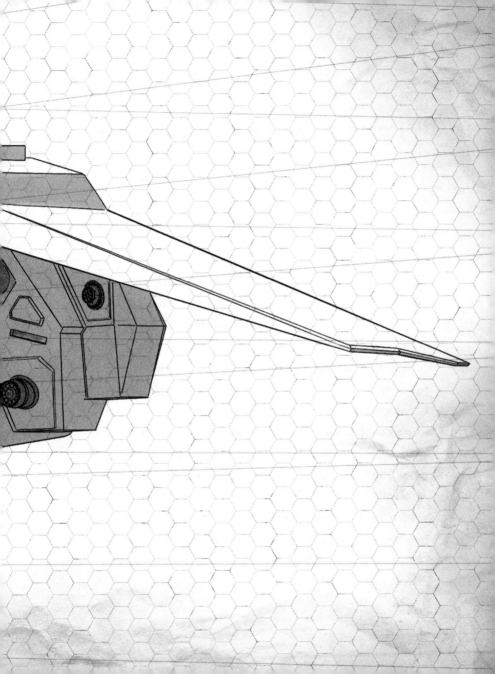

OTHER FORMS OF TRANSPORTATION

THE CHUTES

Moving on from literal wings, let's get into other ways to move. The chutes, aka the pressure elevator, aka the lava chutes, aka that's enough names for the same blasted thing, are the Underground's main route of transportation to the surface. Well, they are now that I've gotten ahold of them, at any rate.

These passageways topside can't be traveled without a protective case (unless you're a troll and don't mind a hearty scalding), as the vents are prone to blasts of high-temperature eruptive air and sometimes a bit of magma flow.

On the surface, these vents are a closely guarded secret, most often located on prime fairy vacation spots, like Tara, Ireland, or Martina Franca, Italy. We've got a few in places like Russia or Los Angeles, as well, but really, who wants to go there? Such a harsh terrain filled with cold, emotionless Mud People who'll do just about anything to survive. And don't get me started on Russia, either!

LAVA
CHUTE

These chutes are all marked E-something-or-other. Chute E18 will get you to Stonehenge in the United Kingdom. Chute E37 leaves you off at Paris, France. You get it. I hope.

But enough about the chutes that nature intended. Let's talk about the part that Foaly intended: the titanium pods.

THE PODS

Constructed by L.E.P. techs but based solely on my designs, of course, these egg-shaped pieces of pure inventive beauty are equipped with a restraining seat and harness, external cameras, an engine with an independent motor in case the vent's compressed air isn't exactly cooperating, and a joystick to help get you where you need to go.

The titanium pods are built with one main goal in mind, and that goal is efficiency. Can't get any better than riding these hotshots at Mach 2 on a tidal flare. Just try to find a quicker way to the surface. I double-horse dare you.

Oh, yeah, Mr. Hotshot. Want to know one thing they're not built for? Comfort!

—HS

TITANIUM POD

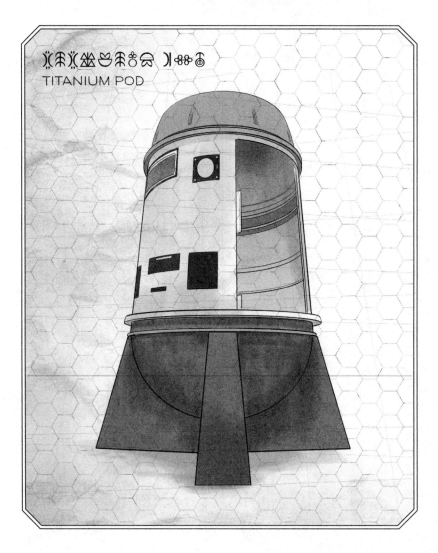

TITANIUM POD
CABIN

RULES FOR PROPER POD SAFETY

◉ Hands and wings inside the pod at all times.

◉ Screaming does not help, so you might as well keep all that to yourself, thank you very much.

◉ In the rare case that you burn up completely, please accept our most humble apologies.

A quick note about the pods. Do not try bringing a Mud Person with you (not that you would want to!). The heat from the pod would easily fry your guest. Fairy lungs are made of stronger stuff, so while it might get warm in there, there's a 99.8 percent chance you'll make it through uncooked.

And, hey, it could be worse. Back when Root was just getting on the force, there weren't even harnesses, cameras, or thrusters built in! I'd say we've made a little progress on that front. (Although some of the active pods have been in service fifty years and are quite due for an upgrade. Did I mention budget cuts already?)

Really, Root? You're going to let him make that dig?

—HS

PRISON TRANSPORT CRAFTS

On the other end of the fun spectrum, you've got prison transport. These reinforced behemoths come chock-full of no fun, with the kinds of bells and whistles that'll have you saying, "Hey, where're all the bells and whistles?"

These big boring blocks are built to do just what the name implies: transport prisoners to and from places like Howler's Peak. Sorry in advance if you get stuck with prison transport. Just know my hooves were tied on this one. Wasn't allowed to take any liberties.

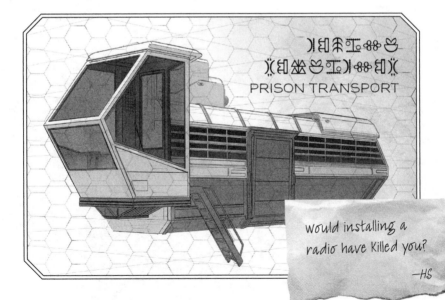

PRISON TRANSPORT

would installing a radio have killed you?

—HS

PRISON TRANSPORT

Prison transport. I'm so glad those days are behind me. I mean, they _are_ behind me, aren't they, Commander? Commander?!?

—Captain Holly Short

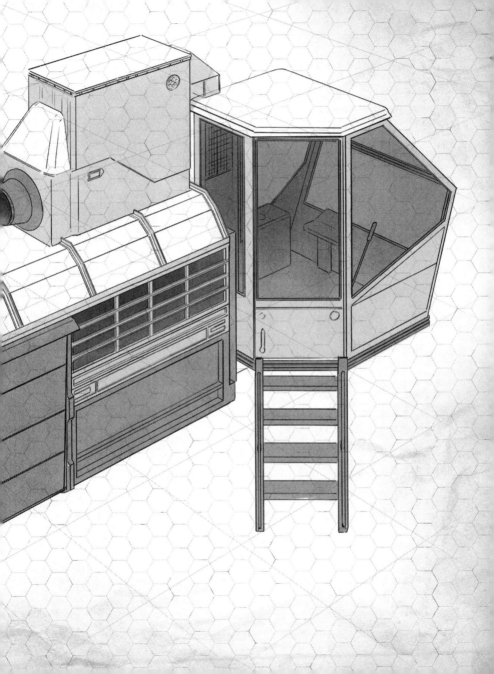

ᚼᚵᚸᚦᚵᚼᚾᚿ
ᚳᚵᚸᚼᚼᛉᛟᛞᚢ
ᚳᚿᛟᛇᚾᚿᚬ

MOBILE
COMMAND
CENTER

MOBILE COMMAND CENTER

Of course there are times when a situation calls for more
officers than our smaller vehicles can carry. That's when we
bring out the big vehicles, like the Mobile Command Center.

The MCC is only really used when we need to set up an
operations point in the field. Our precious Commander Root
can't be shouting orders from the back of a pickup truck, or

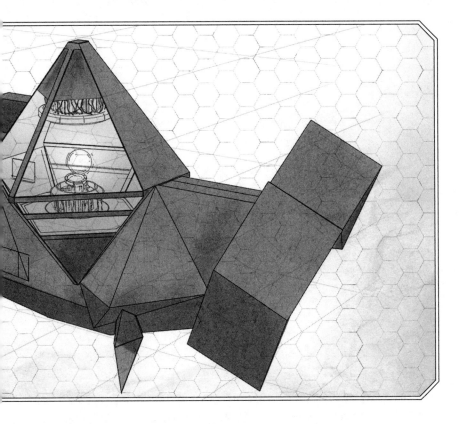

so she tells us. Armed with a laser-proof refractor glass wind-shield and an even tougher body, it is equipped with the most advanced in monitoring and communication gear. We are talking the dream gear. The cream of my technological crop. (Apparently, the budget *is* there for those pieces of equipment that are used to protect the higher-ups.) In any event, the MCC has become a mainstay in large L.E.P. Retrieval operations.

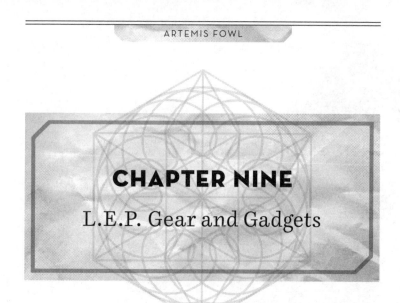

CHAPTER NINE

L.E.P. Gear and Gadgets

Hello. It's me again. Foaly. Just in case it wasn't clear. Nothing worse than digging into a chapter in the old manual and not knowing what voice to imagine floating in your noggin. Well, I guess being eaten by a troll would be worse. Now that I think about it, there are plenty of things worse than not knowing who is narrating a manual. Being stuck behind a dwarf in line for the restroom, attempting to share an ice-cream sundae with a hungry gremlin, waking Commander Root up from her afternoon nap . . .

What were we talking about again? I'm afraid I've lost track.

Oh, yes. Police-issued gear and gadgets. Every one of you rookie officers will get your hands on these beauties. I only make them. It is up to you to use them correctly and stay up-to-date on your training. An officer's weapon is only as strong as the officer's training. (Or so I've been told. I'm not out in the field all that much.)

STANDARD-ISSUE L.E.P. GEAR

THE NEUTRINO 2000

We've got to start somewhere, and the best place to do that is with every officer's first piece of equipment and first line of defense, the Neutrino 2000. The L.E.P. are tasked with the job of protecting and serving, and this handy little zapper helps them do just that.

With settings that range from *fire* (the perfect thing to frighten an uncontrollable dwarf) to *air* (nothing like a blast of pressurized air to knock an elf back to their senses) to *earth* and *water* (also good for a quick drink if you're a bit thirsty on the job), this handy handheld has

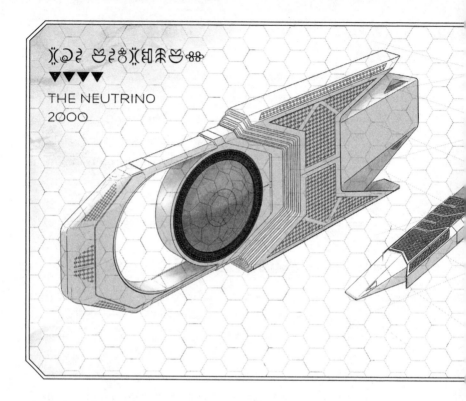

THE NEUTRINO
2000

protected so many L.E.P. officers in the line of duty, I've lost count.

Just switch the dial to your preferred intensity or function, and evildoers usually freeze in their tracks before you even get to hose them down.

Remember, all Neutrinos are nuclear-powered and must be signed out at L.E.P. Headquarters. These aren't your fathers' squirt guns!

ᚠᚷᚦᚦᛁ ᚦᚷᚦᚦᛁᚦ
BOW FORM

ᛏᛁᚷᚦᚦᚷ ᚦᚷᚦᚦᛁᚦ
SWORD FORM

You might want to mention that, left
unchecked, a Neutrino can fill an entire room with
water, as if it were an Olympic-sized swimming pool.
Some of us had to find that out through real-world
experience, but I'm not going to name any names.

(Okay, Root. I can hear your "harrumph." Yes, it
was me.)

—HS

BUZZ BATON

Next up, the buzz baton. Another part of the standard-issue gear for officers, these shocking little numbers are built for sturdy everyday use. Similar in shape and appearance to the wands Mud People officers use, the fairy version is, of course, much more efficient. A baton in working order will run off a battery charge for up to a week. Each officer has their own baton, which is bioconnected to that particular individual. (This was a later design I implemented after far too many instances of innocent bystanders picking up a dropped baton and getting a jolt. Brilliant, if I do say so myself.)

As the name implies, these batons send a buzzing blast of electric energy into any creature they happen to come into contact with—intentionally or by mistake. Nothing like a quick (and mostly harmless) electric jolt to the hind end when a mischievous dwarf tries to pick a pocket or an equally mischievous troll tries to eat a close personal friend.

They're also great for swatting mosquitos on the surface! Not that I would ever do such a thing, because, of course, as this manual says, and the Booke says, we should never interact with things on the surface.

—Captain Holly Short

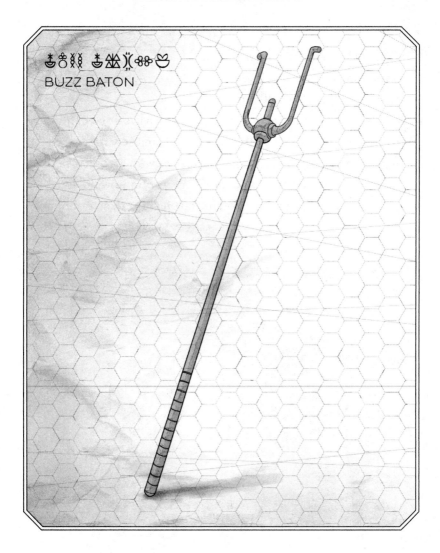

BUZZ BATON

FLIGHT HELMET

Oh, horsefeathers, am I proud of this one. Can't be light on your wings if you can't see where you're going. And that's where *my* flight helmet comes in.

Not only is the helmet equipped with a live-feed camera (on a nuclear battery, so there's no time limit to your recording capabilities), twin five-hundred-kilowatt headlights, a voice-activated communications microphone, and loudspeakers, it is also streamlined for fast flight with an optional

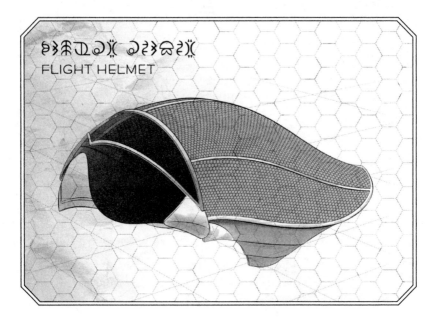

FLIGHT HELMET

mask to filter out harmful pollutants or to supply oxygen at high speeds.

Let's dig into the visor. The first thing you'll notice is that it's quite good at reflecting. Attempts from other fairies to twist your mind or finagle their way out of trouble can be all but ignored when you've got your trusty visor in place.

It's also great for ignoring some of your fellow L.E.P. officers when the room gets a little too raucous or a certain other officer won't stop talking about himself.

—Captain Holly Short

Your visor will also give you infrared, ultraviolet, thermal, and magnified vision when enabled. With this kind of tech, you can see an ant on the nose of a sprite on a moonless night from a mile away, if you're so inclined. The visor is also able to superimpose maps directly on your field of vision, making it virtually impossible to get lost (although Grub Kelp has certainly done his best to prove otherwise). These maps and geographical information can be routed to you directly from our scopes, the trackers I've attached to Mud People's communication satellites.

The fabulous and superpowerful visor aside, the helmet itself is painted with my nearly patented antifriction coating.

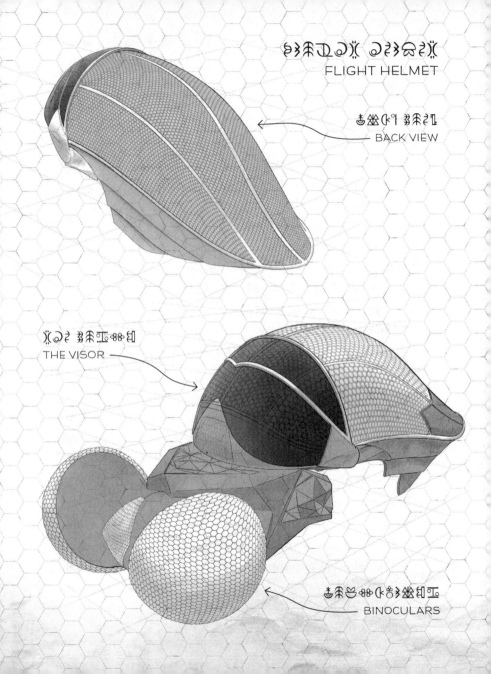

FLIGHT HELMET

← BACK VIEW

THE VISOR —

← BINOCULARS

It offers bursts of emergency high-pitch sonics. It's a decibel too high for humans or elves to detect, yet perfect for driving trolls mad out of their skulls, if that is indeed your intention. The microphone built in, when used in tandem with your L.E.P.-issued earpiece, makes your helmet a one-stop connection to the folks back at headquarters.

These flight helmets are *not* toys. They are works of art. You must treat them with respect. They need routine maintenance. The microphone needs to be cleaned, the paint shined at least two times a week. I did not spend countless hours designing perfection so you could treat it like some inane bicycle helmet. To that end, L.E.P. officers are never permitted to remove their headgear aboveground. This is for your own safety, as well as the safety of the Underground itself. But with all these features and goodies installed, I'm not sure what rational fairy would ever want to take the visor off.

That's because you're not an elf. Flight helmets are murder on my ears. The points always get dry and flaky if I'm topside for too long. Moisturize, elf cadets! It's the only way.

—HS

PERSONAL DEVICES

While the previous pieces of gear are standard to any L.E.P. officer, the following devices are issued upon completing initial training. Rookies—this means you do your job, you get the goodies. Got it?

CONCUSSER

Have a roomful of gnomes you need to incapacitate in a matter of seconds? Find yourself in the middle of a mob of energetic elves who need to take a time-out? Dealing with a dwarf doing destruction and need to stop him ASAP? Then I would recommend the concusser.

This little round device, which fits easily in a pocket, is a handy way of making a small group of fairies go nighty-night

It is very handy. Don't ask how I know. At least not right now. It's been a long day.

—HS

with a quick blast of light. Once you throw it and it starts beeping, don't look directly at it if you value your consciousness. Because with a quick flash, everybody who's watching is going to be out like a light, as the Mud People say.

CONCUSSER

LOCATOR

This watch-sized device has multiple uses. I like to think of it as the centaur of the gadget world. One body, lots of parts. It not only serves as a moonometer—to tell you what time it is—but it's also perfect for tracking and locating a suspect detected by headquarters. One of L.E.P.recon's go-to gizmos, the locator shows your target as a visual blip with an audible *bip* when you're getting closer. Not only that, but it can display maps and magical hot spots.

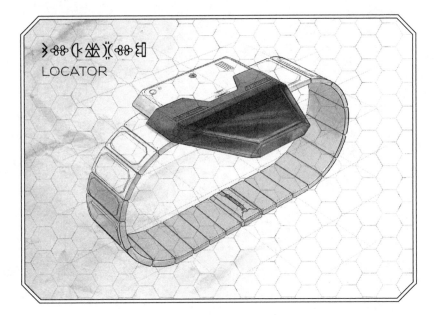

LOCATOR

But perhaps most important, the locator keeps track of your magic power. If you're running hot, it'll let you know. And if you're dangerously low on magic, it'll keep reminding you like an annoying sprite talking about their amazing wings over and over and over again.

Yeah, thanks again for that little feature. Thanks heaps.

—HS

THE "BIG" ONES

Now this manual would not be complete without a look at *all* the gadgets and gear provided to L.E.P. officers. However, as I've mentioned, not all gear is given to all officers. There are some pieces so big, so powerful, so brilliant, so dangerous that only the most skilled officers are allowed access. And even most of those officers—yeah, you know who you are—treat these pieces with respect and a bit of fear. They are powerful. And brilliant. I mentioned that part, right?

MIND-WIPE

Mind-wipe technology is not to be used regularly—or lightly. You can't just go and botch assignment after assignment and hope to wipe the mind of every Mud Person who happens to cross your clumsy path. No, mind-wipes are to be used sparingly, and hopefully not to be used at all. If you're a competent L.E.P. officer, that is.

Hey! I take offense at that!

—HS

Technically speaking, the mind-wipe is a handheld device that is capable of removing specific memories and/or experiences, depending on how the device is set. We used to have to attach electrodes to the temples of the Mud People, but with this advanced model, erasing somebody's recent memories is as easy as using a point-and-shoot camera.

It should never, ever be used on other fairies.

BLUE RINSE

When things are too dangerous or botched for a mind-wipe, there's always the last-resort scenario, the blue rinse. Sounds so innocent, right? But I, for one, don't like to talk much about it. I feel that this ingenious idea of mine was taken and twisted and made into something rather horrible, and I'm offended. And a little bit frightened. If you want to know more about the rinse, ask the Fairy Council, if you're so inclined.

I really wish I never had.

—HS

I'll simply say this devastating biobomb fired from a massive cannon uses a core of solinium 2 to destroy all living tissue in a preset radius in a hail of blue-and-white flame. All with a half-life of fourteen seconds.

There. Now I've said too much. Just hope you never witness it in real life.

TIME FREEZE

Now to completely change the subject. This might be my favorite bit of tech that ever sprang from my genius-level intellect, so pardon me if I go on for a bit. Ever wanted to pause time to take a break? Well, now you can! (Or rather, you can if you have the permission of the majority of the Fairy Council. So in other words, you probably can't.)

A time freeze is a manufactured stop in time in a designated area. This space between seconds is inescapable (well, mostly) and gives the L.E.P. all the time in the world to react to difficult situations.

I first developed this technology when I was studying the ways of warlocks of ancient fairy history. I realized that if we actually stored the magic generated by these types of warlocks, we could unleash their time-halting powers. I even went so far as to develop a time-field portal that allows fairies to enter and exit a time freeze when granted permission by an L.E.P. official.

Now, I'll be the first to say that time freezes aren't perfect. They're far from it, actually. Outside forces like storms and other adverse weather patterns can affect a time

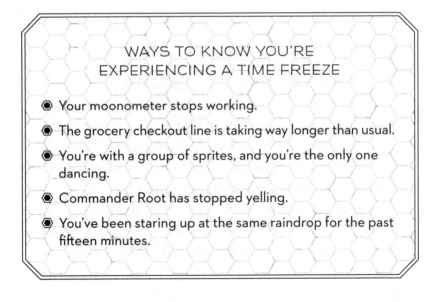

WAYS TO KNOW YOU'RE EXPERIENCING A TIME FREEZE

- Your moonometer stops working.
- The grocery checkout line is taking way longer than usual.
- You're with a group of sprites, and you're the only one dancing.
- Commander Root has stopped yelling.
- You've been staring up at the same raindrop for the past fifteen minutes.

IN A TIME FREEZE, REMEMBER,
BE AWARE!

◎ Rain, dandelion poofs, aloe-filled tissues, and other harmless items can become sharp and splintered when frozen in time!

◎ Those asleep cannot be seen during a time freeze! They disappear. Literally. I'm still working on where they go. Mysteries I cannot solve irk me.

◎ Magical elements can disrupt time freezes if undetected upon activation!

◎ Cats do not like time freezes. They've never said as much, but we just kind of know, you know?

Time can do what now?

—HS

freeze's efficiency. And there's always the risk of a freeze snapping, sending one end of the frozen area colliding with the other. That would result in sending everyone inside the target area spiraling into an inescapable infinite nothingness. But honestly, why worry about the worst-case scenario, yeah?

LITTLE GIZMOS

Not every tool in an L.E.P. officer's belt is substantial in size. But that doesn't mean that they aren't important or valuable in aiding and assisting an officer on the job. Things like hand-cuffs and muzzles (useful for keeping a goblin's fire breath under control) are often invaluable in the field, as is a fun little gadget like a latex finger.

LATEX FINGER

"A latex finger?" I hear you saying to your manual. "What are you going on about now, Foaly?" Well, let me inform you. The latex finger might be the weirdest—but perhaps coolest—tool I've developed to date. It slips comfortably over your actual finger (unless you're a troll or have troll-sized hands) and can usually go undetected by those with lesser intellects. The finger is spring-loaded with exactly one payload: a knockout dart.

"One" being the operative word here, folks. It can fire one dart and one dart only. So make your shot count. It's not like I can afford to arm every one of your digits. An unforeseen, and unfortunate, use for the Latex Finger was discovered when the technology fell into the wrong hands (pun intended). Due to its close fit and the fact that it is made of latex, the finger allows the wearer to hide their fingerprint. This has led to some false arrests and a few cases of B&Es going unsolved. I mention this now not to demonstrate a weakness on the L.E.P.'s part but rather to show that we have to always be thinking one step ahead of the manipulative mind of the criminal.

AHA! I bet you that some officers (not going to mention names) have totally used that trick to snag food that wasn't theirs out of the fridge in the common room!

—Captain Holly Short

IRIS-CAM

Speaking of big devices in small packages, the iris-cam is our eyes in the field. It allows HQ to see what you're seeing, allows you to see better, and can record any important events for posterity. So yeah, make sure you switch the thing off when you're using the loo.

This tiny contact lens is mainly used for covert missions.

IRIS-CAM FUNCTIONS

◉ **ION SENSITIVITY MODE:** View usually undetectable things like camera and laser beams.

◉ **X-RAY MODE:** See the very bones of a building or fairy.

◉ **GLAMOUR FILTER MODE:** Make everybody prettier with a halo of hearts around their heads. (Because who doesn't want the ability to do that?)

Just a hypothetical: If you accidentally dropped your iris-cam down the drain of a water fountain, would the L.E.P. give you a new one?

Root, on a completely unrelated note, the water fountain on level three of Headquarters is clogged. You should probably get maintenance to check that out.

—HS

Not only can we monitor your body's vitals through its precision hardware, but just like a camera, it can also enhance your vision to zoom in on objects. Sure, it might cause you a bit of discomfort, but that's nothing compared with the jolt of pain you'll feel when you're switching between your iris-cam's functions.

(Okay, okay. Nobody is perfect. Not even me. Although I'm as close as you can get. Not bragging. Just statistical fact. There are a few bugs to work out. I'll get to them eventually.)

HOVER TECH—GENERAL

I'm not exactly sure why, but fairies are obsessed with things that hover. I can't tell you how many times a day I get a request for some new bit of hovering technology. Maybe it's because most of us have flight envy these days, being that natural wings are, for most of us, a thing of the past. Maybe it's just the fact that hovering tech looks pretty cool, all things considered. But whatever the reason, I'm constantly bombarded with requests for a hover lounge chair for the break room, or a hover lawnmower for the landscapers, or even more peculiar, a hover toilet for a fellow L.E.P. officer.

If you are taking requests, what about a hover mug— that follows you. I'm always putting down my coffee and losing it. Ha!

—HS

Whatever the case, to most fairies, hovering tech equals better tech, so I developed quite a few vehicles that float just above the ground. I won't get into all of them now, but I'm quite proud of two in particular.

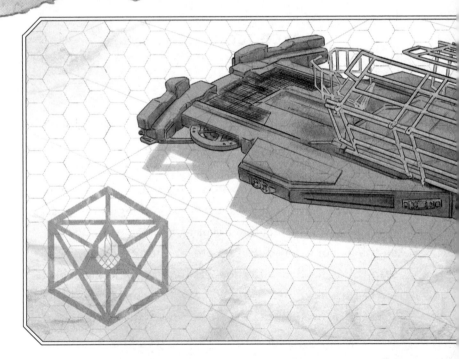

HOVERCAGE

One is the hovercage. It's a cage tough and heavy enough to contain even the most massive troll (it can hold 'em up to sixteen feet tall!). But it still manages to float on a lovely cushion of air. It's one bit of necessary equipment, let me tell you. If the air wasn't doing all the work, I'm not sure the L.E.P. even has enough elves to do that kind of lifting.

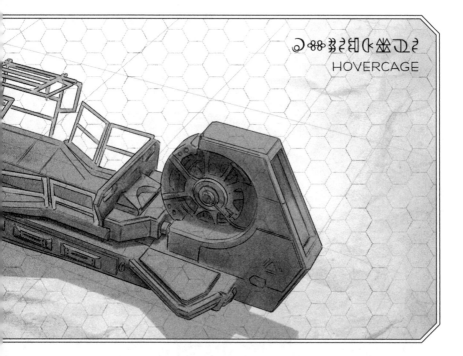

HOVERCAGE

HOVERTROLLEY

A little more for show than efficiency purposes is the hover-trolley. It works on the same basic principles as the hovercage but is designed to carry much, much less. The good thing about this little wagon is that it can be driven remotely with a trackpad. It also has an automatic clearance compensator

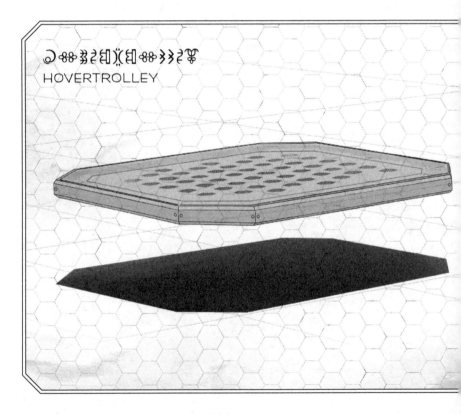

HOVERTROLLEY

to help it navigate up and down stairs and is equipped with a fish-eye camera. Now it doesn't quite handle like I'd like it to yet, but the camera is a great feature. With its instant feed, I can see exactly who is laughing at the hovertrolley and for what duration. We'll see if you get what you ask for next time you come knocking on my door, Chix.

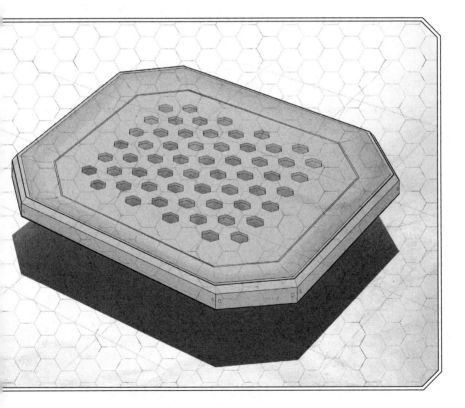

Do you remember the time the hovertrolley got stuck on that escalator in New York City? Oh, man, it tripped so many tourists that day. I still watch that camera feed on a weekly basis.

—HS

Well, I think I should bring this section to a close (though I'm sure it has been your favorite). Root gave me a certain page count to stay below, and let's just say I blew past that by the time I started talking about the flight helmets. What can I say? I love my work.

Here's hoping that you lot enjoy your time in the L.E.P. just as much.

Or at least the first few centuries. That is the honeymoon period, after all.

And just in case you missed the many, many reminders I put in my section—this gear is not a toy. Not even the gear that may *look* like a toy. I have the authority to take any and all items away from officers not following protocol. Don't make me be the bad guy, here. I just want to invent. And talk about my inventing.

CHAPTER TEN

Cautionary Tale #3

TALE #3 TAKEAWAY:
AN L.E.P. OFFICER
MUST FULLY UNDERSTAND AND
MAINTAIN POLICE-ISSUED EQUIPMENT.

Commander Root again. This last procedure lesson hits close to home, and that's mostly because it happened to me. I filled out this report over five hundred years ago, when I was just an officer, not even a captain yet. But the events it describes are still etched into my mind as if they happened last week. I guess some memories are like that.

LOWER ELEMENTS POLICE
OFFICER INCIDENT REPORT

INITIAL REPORT: #009-4691-888-23

STATEMENT BY: OFFICER ROOT

LOCATION: POLICE HEADQUARTERS, HAVEN CITY

Officer Blump and I arrived at 18 Pennywonk Way at approximately 02:00 hours. It seemed like a routine call at first. Some neighbors had reported a noise disturbance coming from the thirteenth floor of a large apartment complex. A goblin party had been carrying on until early in the morning, and one concerned citizen just wanted to get some sleep. She reported loud music and chanting, and the occasional burst of flame out an open window. Like I said, routine.

As soon as we got there, I should have realized that something was off.

"Are we sure this is the place?" Blump said. He wasn't acting like the overly confident partner I'd known for the past ten months. He seemed nervous, which was something I didn't even know he could be.

"'Eighteen Pennywonk,'" I read on the outside of the large double doors. To be sure, I even pointed the number out to him. I find it is always better to err on the side of caution when dealing with anyone—even my own partner. "We're here, all right."

Sounds like you were a blast at parties even back then. Kidding! Don't fire me!!

—HS

Blump made a weird noise and then shrugged. I walked up to the building and rang the buzzer of the apartment in question: 13X. There was no answer. Since the music was loud enough to drown out most casual conversations down there on the street, I knew the complaint was legit. So when they ignored the buzzer a few more times, I tried 13Y. The tenant of that apartment was more than glad to let the L.E.P. inside the building. Anything to finally get some sleep, I'm sure.

I went into the building first, with Blump reluctantly shuffling in behind me. He certainly wasn't the wishy-washy sort before, so this behavior struck me as odd. Officer Baron Blump was a good cop, the way I saw it. Sure, he was a bit lazy when it came to filing paperwork or paying attention at police workshops. He often did the bare minimum of what was expected of him when it came to maintaining his gear or fueling up his energy reserves. But he had always had my back, even in some of the toughest scrapes a fairy can imagine. When you face a pack of rampaging trolls with a fellow officer, you're bonded for life.

But this particular night—well, morning, really—he was acting very . . . peculiar, to say the least.

By the time we got to the thirteenth floor—it was a walk-up, if you can believe that—I had worked myself up to a suitable level of anger. These goblins couldn't be bothered to keep their volume at a reasonable level, so I had to be bothered to hike a mountain of a stairwell just to tell them to keep it down. It's enough to make any well-intentioned L.E.P. officer irate. So when we got to 13X, I didn't just knock on the door, I pounded on it.

"What?" came a voice from behind the peephole.

"L.E.P.," I said. "Open up."

The goblin behind the door didn't answer at first. And then the music, which had just been literally shaking the light fixtures in the hallway, suddenly shut off.

"No one's home," the goblin finally said.

"You realize I am talking to you," I said, "so I know some-one is there?"

"Oh," said the goblin. "Well, I'm not home any longer. I've gone out."

"Open the door," I repeated. I took a moment and glanced back at Blump. He was fidgeting with his belt. One hand was on his Neutrino holster, and the other hand was on the belt loop that held his buzz baton. I could almost see his palms sweating from where I was standing.

The goblin realized he'd been severely outwitted. That doesn't take much where goblins are concerned, of course, but either way, he cracked open the door.

"There," he said. "I've opened the door. Now if you'll excuse me, I have to get back to studying for my university exam."

"Could you open the door a bit further?" I asked. I wasn't really asking, and he could tell that from my tone of voice.

The goblin thought about this for a second, and then he tried to slam the door shut. Luckily, I have a pretty quick foot. Sure, it hurt a little to shove my boot in the crack as he slammed it, but it kept the door from locking.

"I've gone out again!" the goblin shouted.

"I can see you!" I said. "You haven't gone anywhere!"

"Where should I stack the dynamite?" came another voice from deeper inside the apartment.

I looked at the goblin and he looked back at me.

"That was the radio," he said. But I'd heard enough. Without glancing at Blump, I put my shoulder to the door and knocked it wide open. The goblin fell to the ground in front of me, but I wasn't looking at him any longer. I was looking at a roomful of goblins and stacks and stacks of Mud People-made dynamite. Not only was this an apartment full of illegal human contraband, it was full of deadly contraband at that.

One of the goblins near the back of the group began to form a fireball in his hand.

"No!" yelled one with a large scar down his cheek. He seemed to be the leader. "Fireballs out the window only! You want the whole place to blow?"

That was a good sign. I had them at a disadvantage. I pulled my Neutrino 2000 from my holster and quickly switched the dial to *water*. The water function was always a good one to handle goblins. It was even better when you wanted to keep dynamite from catching on fire and exploding.

"Nobody move!" I yelled. And to my relief, none of the goblins did. Someone did move, however. Behind me, I heard the rustling of Blump's loose-fitting uniform as he pulled his buzz baton out of his belt loop. I could see him a bit out of the corner of my eye, and I remember thinking it was odd that he was going for his baton rather than his Neutrino. But when I felt the shock of electricity coursing through my system, everything started to make sense.

Oh, no! Not Blump!
Anyone but Blump!

—HS

When I woke up, I was tied to a chair, my hands bound behind me. A stack of dynamite was neatly organized in a pile to my right. The goblins had fled the scene, leaving only Blump and me in the dingy apartment.

"So I take it you know these guys," I said when I found the energy to speak.

Blump didn't answer. He was too busy fidgeting with his Neutrino. He had the gun pointed right at the dynamite. I could see that the dial was set on *fire*.

"Let me guess," I said. "You've been turning a blind eye to the activities of these goblins. Maybe you've even been helping them smuggle their dynamite into the city. All for a cut of the take. But you didn't expect to have your operation blown wide open because your goblin buddies are too stupid to keep it down when they're sorting their contraband."

"That's the long and short of it," said Blump. He didn't look me in the eye. At least he had the sense to seem ashamed.

"So now what?" I asked. But I already knew what he had planned.

"I'm going to light that fuse and skedaddle," he said, nodding to the long fuse sticking out of the dynamite pile. I wasn't sure that even a fuse like that would buy him the time he needed to run down thirteen flights of stairs, but I figured Blump knew more about this stuff than I did. Who knows how many hours he'd spent working with the goblins and their dynamite?

Blump, however, was careless as usual. He had made sure he'd taken my Neutrino and buzz baton, but he hadn't done a thorough inspection of the rest of my person. That's standard L.E.P. procedure when restraining a suspect. But like I said, Blump was lazy about that sort of thing. That meant he hadn't noticed I had a pocketknife in the back pouch of my belt. While we'd been talking, I had popped it out and had been sawing at my ropes for almost a full minute already.

He must have realized I was up to something, because Blump suddenly raised his Neutrino from the dynamite to me.

"What are you up to?" he asked. He sounded more than nervous. He sounded panicked.

"Now, Blump, just take it easy," I said.

But he didn't. Instead, he pulled the trigger. But nothing happened. Of course nothing happened. Blump had forgotten to charge his Neutrino. Like I said, careless.

The rope snapped just in time. Blump was too busy smacking the side of his Neutrino to see me leap toward him. In seconds, I had tackled him and cuffed him. I gave the dynamite a quick dousing with the water spray from my Neutrino, just to be on the safe side. Then I read Blump his rights as I marched him down the stairs.

I brought him back here to Police Headquarters, and that was that. Now if you'll excuse me, I'm still on the clock. I've got a pack of goblins to track down. And don't worry, my equipment is recharged and ready to use. I'm no Blump.

Wow! I remember hearing about that goblin bust! That's how you made captain. Is that where the expression "Don't pull a Blump!" came from? I always wondered about that when I heard it at the academy. Now I know. Look at that! This manual really is full of helpful tidbits.

That was a compliment, in case you missed it, Root! Just another reason not to fire me. Please!

—HS

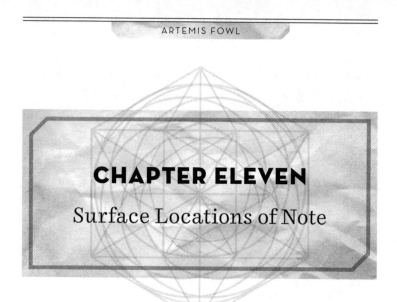

CHAPTER ELEVEN

Surface Locations of Note

As a member of the L.E.P., you'll spend the bulk of your time underground. As commander, I spend more time than I'd like topside, but even I find that I take most of my meals by the twilight of Haven City rather than in the light of the sun or the moon. I'm rarely aboveground more than a few hours at a time, but still, it's enough to make me worried about exposure to the many pollutants the Mud People keep unleashing on the planet.

In the event that you do venture aboveground, whether it be on a L.E.P.recon scouting mission, an L.E.P. Retrieval operation, or just a magic renewal holiday, there are a handful of surface locations that every L.E.P. officer *must* be familiar with.

FAIRY FORTS

There are a lot of these little dwellings hidden all over Earth, so I'm just going to give you a general overview. If I started listing the pros and cons of one fairy fort over another, this book would look less like an official L.E.P. manual and more like the ElfAdvisor website.

Fairy forts are ancient structures and our portal to the outside world. They used to be our main place of dwelling, but that was before the Mud People forced us deeper underground. These days, chutes often end at, or near, a fort, and the bigger forts are strategically placed. The forts are found near magical hubs around the planet, or close to important human cities that the L.E.P. may need to patrol from time to time. Don't expect much technology in these primitive locations. Just a few external monitors for security purposes and a self-destruct device in case a human gets too close to discovering our secrets.

Fairy forts can sometimes be tough to navigate. After all, you're looking at a place that serves as a hub for official police business but is also a tourist destination and an emergency shelter for a fairy in need. Because of all this, it is vital that fairy forts remain hidden from human beings. Too much of our culture can be learned just by observing the many fairies who come and go from these busy areas. It's for this reason that most fairy forts

IS MY FAIRY FORT ABOUT TO SELF-DESTRUCT?

- ◎ Do you hear a grating alarm, like a foghorn stuck in a blender?

- ◎ Are red lights flashing overhead?

- ◎ Do you feel a slight rumble in the ground beneath your feet?

- ◎ Are the fairies around you screaming or saying things like "Well, this place is about to self-destruct"?

- ◎ If you answered yes to any of these questions, then there's a good chance your fairy fort is about to self-destruct.

- ◎ If you're still reading this, there's also a fairly decent chance that you're about to self-destruct with it.

- ◎ For fairy's sake! Stop reading and run!

are elegantly camouflaged. It's our intention to make sure the forts look like not much more than a simple mound of earth if a Mud Person drops by unexpectedly. However, some artsy-fartsy types have gone and all but made that impossible in some places. Case in point: Tara.

I hope there are no "artsy-fartsy" types reading this manual, Commander Root. Or you've certainly offended them.

—HS

TARA

Ireland is the favored destination of most fairy folk; however, most fairies know this ancient and magical land by its name in the old tongue, Éiriú. This old country is the one spot on Earth where humans are most in tune with magic. They're more inclined to live in harmony with a fairy if they catch a passing glimpse of one, and more adult Mud People believe in us here than anywhere else. The children are believers in even higher numbers.

It was in Ireland ten thousand years ago that the ancient fairy race—the Dé Danann—battled the demon

HILL OF TARA

Fomorians, carving the famous Giants' Causeway with their magical blasts. This land is home to the Lia Fáil, the rock at the center of the very universe where fairy kings were crowned. It is a grand place of tradition and the number one box every fairy tourist wants to check off.

The most magical spot in Ireland is Tara, a hot spot for all breeds of vacationers. Six shuttles per week head to Tara from Haven City alone. Chute E1 is always crammed with those wishing for a magical recharge. And yes, full moons at Tara are a mix of a congestion nightmare and a partier's dream. The fairy fort located there even has a fully equipped passenger lounge, something most forts could never afford.

Tara is a lovely place, even with its overly designed rock formations that surely will alert more humans to our presence one of these days. Its spring water is the most refreshing I've ever personally tasted and can easily restore a fairy's youth. The water is also known to cure a bellyful of holy water on occasion. (Why kids these days keep attempting the so-called "Holy Water Challenge," I'll never know. That kind of stunt is just reckless. It can make an officer's routine station at the fort a nightmare—trust me.)

The only main drawback of Tara is that it's nestled right next to one of the most dangerous locations on the planet: Fowl Manor.

I was wondering when you were going to get to it. Took you long enough.

—HS

FOWL MANOR

Near Tara, in the heart of County Meath, Ireland, stands a structure that is strictly off-limits to any and all L.E.P. personnel. I cannot stress this enough. Only under my direct command may any L.E.P.recon or Retrieval officer set foot on the grounds of Fowl Manor. And even then, L.E.P. officers should make it quick. Fowl Manor is not a place for photo ops, no matter how impressive its architecture. It's not a place to dawdle or to stop for a picnic. It's not even a place to fly over. You fly *around* Fowl

Manor. Is that clear? If I catch wind of any stunts pulled with Fowl's foul manor, you will be terminated. On the spot. Again, do I make myself clear?

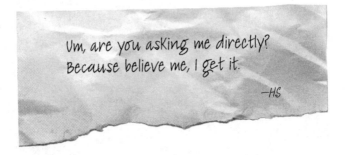

Um, are you asking me directly? Because believe me, I get it.

—HS

Fowl Manor is located on a two-hundred-acre estate outside Dublin. The mansion was built by Lord Hugh Fowl in the fifteenth century. Even by fairy standards, it's an impressive structure. Its halls are full of deep mysteries that would capture even the most reserved elf's curiosity. The portrait gallery alone is fascinating in its artistry. So much so that if invited in, a fairy might be tempted to just take a quick lap through—

No! Don't even think about it! That was a test, and you failed, Officer!

Because if you do take that quick lap, you'll also quickly discover that no cost was spared to keep Fowl

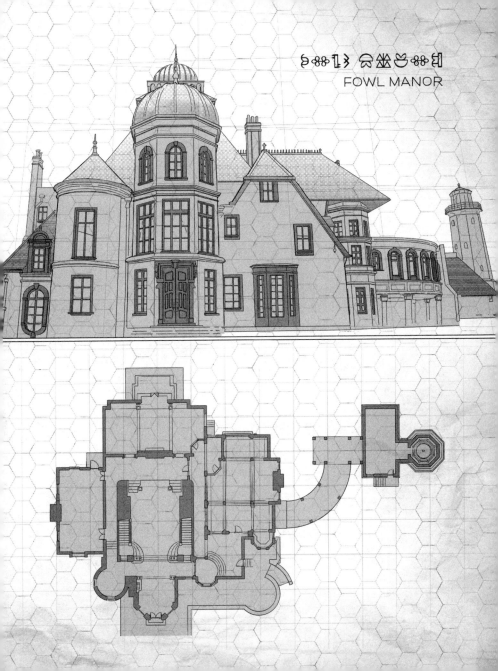

FOWL MANOR

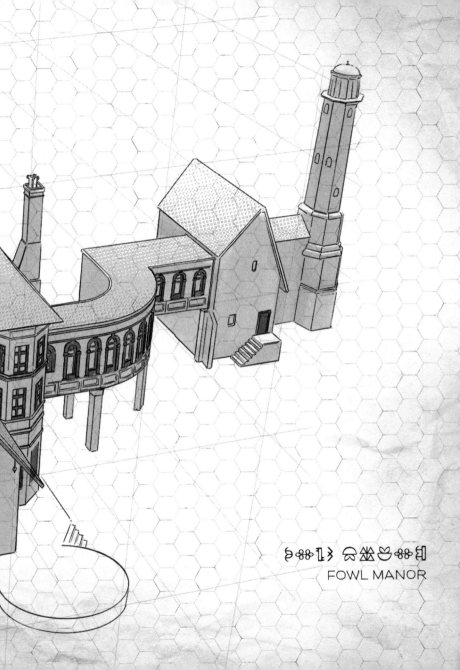

FOWL MANOR

Manor equipped with the best and most advanced surveillance equipment, security and personal. A normal

SURFACE VISITOR CHECKLIST

So you're headed to the surface? Here's a handy checklist of items to bring to make your holiday as magical as possible:

- ◉ Toothbrush and toothpaste
- ◉ Underwear
- ◉ Socks
- ◉ Extra underwear
- ◉ Protein bars
- ◉ Moonometer

- ◉ Nettle shakes
- ◉ Moonblock lotion
- ◉ Passport
- ◉ More underwear (you'd be surprised)
- ◉ A positive attitude!

But just to be clear, do NOT visit Fowl Manor, right? Just checking. Not being snarky. Promise!

—HS

wall can hide a dozen scan-
ners that can instantly alert
the necessary Mud People
of your presence. And don't
get me started on a certain
young Fowl's ability to take
our own equipment and use
it against us.

I can't help feeling this whole section is very pointed. . . .

—HS

As an L.E.P. officer, you need to keep in mind one main thing about all surface locations: fairies no longer belong topside. As hypnotic as the unfiltered air and moonlight can be, Earth's surface is no longer our home. Never forget that.

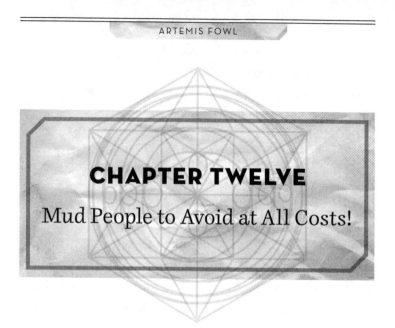

CHAPTER TWELVE
Mud People to Avoid at All Costs!

There are those who think I'm being dramatic when they hear me talk about the most dangerous men and women on the planet. They think I'm employing hyperbole and exaggerating just how detrimental these Mud People are to the safety of our people. Let's just say that those who doubt this dire threat fall into two columns: fairies who have been fired from the L.E.P. and fairies who are about to be fired from the L.E.P.

So take this list seriously, Officer.

ARTEMIS
FOWL JR.

Oooh, I can't stand that smug face! Do we have to include it? I mean, yes, we are technically sort-of allies now, but, ugh, it just gets me sometimes.

—HS

ARTEMIS FOWL JR.

This is the big one, and sure, that sounds a little strange seeing as how by human standards he's not that big at all. Artemis Fowl Jr. is a young boy. He's a virtual baby in fairy terms, and not much more than that in Mud People vernacular, either. However, he's also the only human being I'm aware of in recent centuries who has gained his own copy of *The Booke of the People*. Not only that, but he figured out a way to read it, thereby unlocking *all* its secrets. He now has a vast understanding of our language, culture, and traditions. I'd wager he knows more about fairies than you, whoever you may be.

The trouble with this kid is that he's a genius. And not just a genius but a genius with a vast fortune. The Fowl family has a long and infamous lineage, dating back centuries. They've grown accustomed to wealth and power, and for whatever reason, Artemis Fowl Jr. craves more of both.

Now some of my officers—mainly Captain Holly Short—claim that Artemis has good intentions behind his plotting and scheming. But I find it hard to understand

Hey, I'm not defending him! This kid gets under my skin more than anyone I've ever met!

—HS

the motives of a child who has no qualms about kidnapping fairy folk.

Long story short—no offense, Holly—avoid Artemis Fowl as if your very life depends on it. Because it just might.

None taken. Well, maybe a little was taken. Just a little though. I get it. Sort of.

—Captain Holly Short

DOMOVOI BUTLER

From what I understand, Domovoi Butler is just one Butler in a long line of Butlers. Do not be fooled by the name. The Butlers do not . . . buttle. They are protectors and bodyguards, each protecting their particular charge in the Fowl family.

The current Butler is a force to be reckoned with— or rather not reckoned with. He should be avoided. Remember?

With a penchant for a Mud Person gun called a Sig Sauer and a fierce loyalty to Artemis Fowl Jr., Butler is a highly trained, very powerful individual who is easily capable of defeating even the most well-trained L.E.P. officer. Butler's only weakness is his niece—Juliet.

DOMOVOI
BUTLER

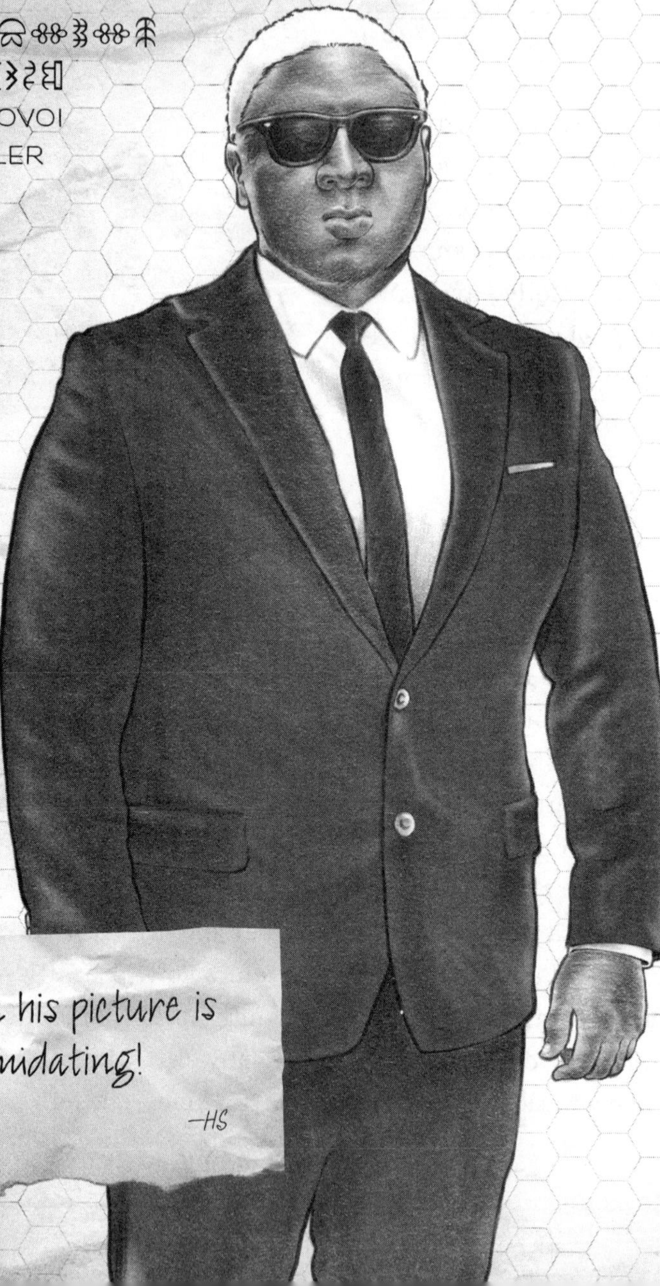

Even his picture is
intimidating!

—HS

JULIET

Juliet is Butler's niece and a force to be reckoned with in her own right. Trained by her uncle, Juliet is an expert sword fighter, martial artist, and archer, and a fan of something the Mud People call pro wrestling.

JULIET

Like Artemis Fowl Jr., Juliet can easily be under-estimated. Don't trust that sweet smile! While I'm not sure the exact relationship she has to Artemis, she seems to be special to the boy. But if I had to guess, I'd bet that Artemis isn't big in the friend department and probably treasures anyone who comes close to being one.

ANGELINE FOWL

As little as we know about the rest of the residents of Fowl Manor, we know even less about Artemis's mother, Angeline Fowl. There are rumors that she suffers from depression. Some say she suffers from dementia. Some say she doesn't suffer at all, except by being the mother of a criminal ne'er-do-well.

However, even more than Juliet, Angeline might be the weak point in the armor Artemis Fowl has built around himself. Every boy, even one as misguided as Artemis Fowl, loves his mother.

That last sentence implies that Artemis has a heart. Are we sure that's true? I mean, has it been scientifically proven?

—HS

ANGELINE
FOWL

ARTEMIS FOWL SR.

As it turns out, young Artemis isn't the only Fowl to study the ways of the People. His father made quite a hobby of it and was the main source of inspiration when Artemis Fowl Jr. decided to try to hunt down some fairy gold of his own.

In his day, Artemis Fowl Sr. seemed to consider himself a bit of a Robin Hood, to borrow a figure from Mud People legends. He routinely located stolen money and took it back from the corrupt. However, this bizarre method of accumulating wealth didn't begin with Fowl Sr. In fact, it's a longstanding tradition in the Fowl lineage.

Artemis Fowl Sr. seems to be off the chessboard as of late. Some time ago, he disappeared while aboard a tanker called the *Fowl Star*. However, we should still consider him a very dangerous adversary of the People. He is more experienced than—and perhaps just as well versed in our lore and history as—his son and must be viewed as a dire threat to our continued way of life.

It's essential to remember that every single Mud Person should be avoided. Not just the few mentioned in this chapter. But in the rare and

One Artemis Fowl is bad enough. Can you imagine two?

—HS

I'm surprised, given the, um, connection to Artemis Sr. and my dad, that you would include a picture of the most important piece of fairy treasure ever lost—and then found. But like I've said, your manual, your rules.

—HS

unfortunate case that you should encounter any of the notorious Fowl family, keep in mind that traditional weapons against Mud People may not be effective. The Fowls and the Butlers now know all about the People, and no amount of Mesmer or mind-wiping can change that.

So keep your distance when the Fowls are involved, and just hope it's not your magic they're after.

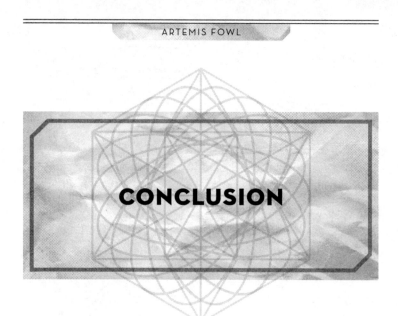

CONCLUSION

Well, that's it for this manual. But this is certainly not all I have to say about working in the Lower Elements Police force. Really, this book barely scratches the surface. As Captain Short would no doubt tell you, I'm a by-the-book commander, and that means constantly reminding my staff about the rules and how to go about following them.

It's my hope that you've learned something by reading and rereading this text. (You better have read it cover to cover, Officer! Twice! At least!) Sure, you probably garnered significantly less information from

Foaly's chapters, but that's to be expected. With any luck, this book has been an informative resource for how an L.E.P. officer conducts him or herself. It has hopefully reminded you not just of our rules and regulations, but of why you wanted to be an L.E.P. officer in the first place.

The world is a much more dangerous place than it was even a few short years ago. More and more Mud People seem to be learning of the existence of the People every day. The only thing that stands between a devastating war between the Mud People and the fairy folk is the L.E.P. We're the few, the brave, and the proud. We're the last magical line of defense keeping the Underground safe.

I began this book with a quote from *The Booke of the People.* So I'll end it with my own paraphrasing of that important text:

But, Fairy, remember this above all:
I am not for those in mud that crawl.
And forever doomed shall be the one
Who doesn't listen to Commander Root.
(I'm the boss. I don't need to rhyme.)

Commander Root

L.E.P. HEADQUARTERS, HAVEN CITY

Overall, this was a pretty good first draft. I give it four out of five stars. It'd be a five out of five if you talked more about my impeccable flight record, or at least mentioned my adorable wit and charm. But, hey, maybe you can fit all that in on the next pass.

In the meantime, were you serious about going to Spud's? I'm starving. Also, you're buying. Hey, I read your book, didn't I? I deserve <u>something</u> in return!

—Captain Holly Short

ADDENDUM

GNOMMISH-TO-ENGLISH TRANSLATION KEY

LETTERS

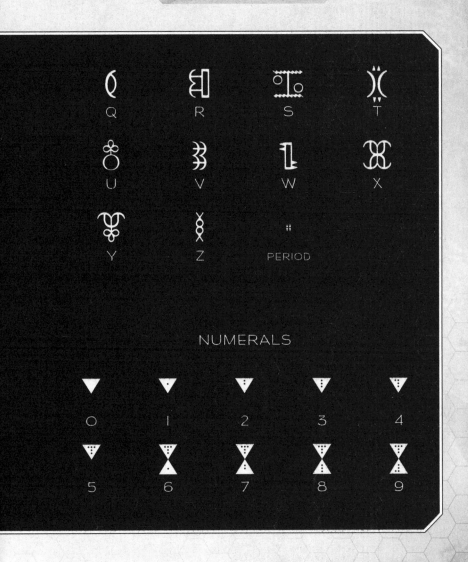

Q

R

S

T

U

V

W

X

Y

Z

PERIOD

NUMERALS

0

1

2

3

4

5

6

7

8

9